What th

MW00415550

R.G. Ryan's stories never fail to open up my own private world, to show me people I ignore every day in all their splendid humanity. Read them. You know you want to.

—Scott Lawson, Hartville, MO, Teacher

One of R.G. Ryan's greatest gifts is his astute observation of the workaday world. While sitting in a coffee shop, he is able to filter daily life and bring to light the humor, the poignancy, and the goodness found therein.

—April Gardner, Chicago, IL, Editor

Reading RG is like people-watching in the company of a particularly observant and articulate friend.

—Rebecca Smith, Manchester, England, Journalist

If, like me, you live in the real world but still endeavor to appreciate life's countless merits, be sure to pick up this book. The ponderings contained herein will both enlighten and entertain you.

—Kirk Starr, Seattle, WA, Graphic Designer

Snapshots at St. Arbuck's deftly captures quiet, personal human moments in one of the least likely of places—a bustling coffee shop. R.G. Ryan's observations and vignettes remind us that there are stories unfolding in front of us constantly and that perhaps all we need to do is sit still for a minute to hear and see them.

—Steve Betz, San Diego, CA, Scientist

R.G Ryan's musings are a delightful read, a warm perspective on a microcosmic 'going-for-coffee population,' which can oftentimes be representative of all humanity.

—Patricia Volonaikis Davis, Northern California, Author

I love walking in to the conceptual *St. Arbuck's* and finding out what new observation or experience R.G. Ryan has to talk about.

—Joseph Hampel, Carlsbad, CA, College Student

Snapshots At St. Arbuck's reminds me of "This American Life"—it takes the ordinary, everyday occurrences and makes them extraordinary. R.G. Ryan has a way of seeing the universe that is unique and his voice is clear and inviting.

—Randee Dawn, North America, Journalist

R.G. Ryan has opened my eyes to the heretofore faceless throng I walk amongst every day. His observations are both poignant and pointed. Quite simply they build my faith in the human race.

—James Parks, Utah, Photographer, Beekeeper

The ratio between complete drivel and worthy writing is something like 1,000,000,000:1. R.G. Ryan helps keep this precarious ratio from falling into oblivion.

—Daniel Brian Abbey, Manila, Philippines, Writer

Snapshots At St. Arbuck's™

Snapshots

At

St. Arbuck's™

Hijacked By Hope In A
Neighborhood Coffee Bar

R.G. Ryan

COPYRIGHT © 2008 by R.G. Ryan.

All rights reserved. This book or parts thereof may not
be reproduced in any form, stored in a retrieval system,
or transmitted in any form by any means—electronic,
mechanical, photocopy, recording, or otherwise—without
prior written permission of the publisher, except as provided
by United States of America copyright law.

This book is a work of fiction. Names, characters, places and
incidents are products of the author's imagination.
Any resemblance to actual events or persons, living or dead,
is purely coincidental.

Published by Dream Chasers Media Group, LLC
Las Vegas, NV

dreamchasersmedia@gmail.com

Library of Congress Control Number 2008933977

ISBN: 978-0-9817581-0-7

For Cheri

Contents

Foreword

I don't drink coffee. I tried it once when I was a kid and it tasted awful. I don't even like coffee ice cream, so I'm not a regular at Starbuck's, although I'm an admirer of Howard Schultz and the whole organization. It's one of the greatest companies anywhere.

I occasionally cross the threshold at Starbucks, however, because they have good, cold milk and delicious blueberry muffins. I usually get them to go, as I'm a little self-conscious sipping milk in a Starbucks. After reading R.G. Ryan's *Snapshots At St. Arbuck's*, I'm going to change my strategy, because I love to watch people and contemplate life. I don't think I'll ever do it as well as R.G., but he has inspired me to sit around Starbucks and give it a try.

I started to read *Snapshots* on a plane ride from Amsterdam to Barcelona and couldn't put it down. When I got to my hotel, I had to finish it. Socrates once said, "An unexamined life is not worth living." Well, R.G. Ryan would make Socrates smile. This little book will make you think about every part of your life: your childhood, important adults (like parents, grandparents, aunts and uncles, relationships) your career, your future—you name it, it comes to life under R.G.'s observant eye. And does he express his observations well! I was jealous of his writing as I was reading. I am a raving fan of R.G. and this book.

Snapshots At St. Arbuck's will take you more than a minute to read, but it's worth every second. Let R.G. Ryan put your life into perspective. While I recently celebrated the forty-seventh anniversary of my twenty-first birthday, I am pumped up about what lies ahead. I always thought that the best was yet to come—but now I am excited about being a participant observer of it. Thanks, R.G.

—Ken Blanchard, co-author of *The One Minute Manager®* and *Leading at a Higher Level*

Introduction

SAINT Arbuck is the little known, yet beloved patron saint of coffee drinkers. And regardless of the sign over the door or the color of apron worn by the baristas, wherever coffee is served and people congregate it *is* St. Arbuck's for homage is dutifully and thankfully paid to his beneficence.

And while I have absolutely no proof to back this up, other than my own powers of observation, I have come to believe that virtually everything significant in life happens sooner or later in a neighborhood coffee bar. By simply sitting quietly and surveying the ever-changing human drama against this backdrop, you can learn quite a lot about yourself and the other folks who cohabit the planet.

Most days you can find me so occupied. I sit. Sip. Converse with friends. I watch. Listen. And on those rare occasions when good story presents itself, I write it down. This book is a sort of chicken soup for the caffeine crowd. Random snapshots of real life...real people as viewed through the eyes of hope.

Hope.

Some find it in perilously short supply these days. Within the pages of this book, it is my intent to lead you on a treasure hunt, for hope can be found in abundance if you know where to look.

So, come take a look at my collection of snapshots.

You may see a picture of someone you know.

You may see a picture of yourself.

Or, you may just want to enjoy looking around.

Oh, and if you want to buy me a cuppa' Joe while you're at it, I won't turn you down.

1

Saint Arbuck

IT was a lazy Monday morning and I decided to get out of the house and pay a visit to the patron saint of coffee drinkers, Saint Arbuck at one of the many, uh, cathedrals scattered across the Las Vegas valley.

It was a beautiful morning in Las Vegas and as I creamed and sweetened my coffee, I sensed the patio beckoning.

Just as I started to exit, I noticed a young father making his way across the patio grasping a baby carrier with one hand while pushing a double stroller with the other.

He approached the double doors of the entryway with visible apprehension as if unused to dealing with a challenge of such magnitude.

Suddenly, I forgot all about the patio and found myself settling in at a table that provided a good view.

I figured that observing how he handled ordering coffee while at the same time dealing with two year-old twins and a tiny baby would be worth delaying my patio time.

I was right. The resulting show played out in three segments:

1. Waiting in line.
2. Ordering.
3. Exiting.

Waiting in line required constant wrangling of the twins who seemed driven by the belief that everything within reach demanded their touch.

Everything.

Bags of coffee; cups; CD's; books; coffee makers; newspapers left behind on chairs.

You get the picture.

Kristen and Kirsten were the names of the little darlings.

I'm not kidding.

"Kristen, put that cup down; Kirsten, give that man his paper; Kristen, don't drop that bag of...can somebody tell the manager that there's a spill out here?"

Like that.

At the same time the infant, who had been asleep, awoke with a bombastic pronouncement of his displeasure.

There is an opera company somewhere in the future who may want to look this young man up.

Once at the counter, the ordering process was chaotic, what with the infant's raucous complaining, the twins unintelligible chatter amidst the usual din of noise that comes from behind the counter.

To my surprise, he ordered multiple drinks, which added another element of difficulty, i.e. how to transport the drinks when his hands were already full.

It was at this point that I almost began to pity the poor guy.

Almost.

As the barista sat the three drinks on the coffee bar, panic seemed to seize him as he realized his dilemma.

He looked at the drinks, at the stroller, at the door, back to the drinks, over to the condiment table, back to the drinks and then stood in one place as if paralyzed by indecision.

By this time, I'd ceased to enjoy the spectacle and stepped forward to offer my assistance.

"Thanks," he said with genuine gratitude, "but I really need to learn how to do this."

"First time alone?" I inquired.

He nodded his head while blowing out a long breath of air and widening his eyes.

"My wife is out of town until Friday."

I had to compress my lips to hide a smile.

"Wow," I said. "You believe in prayer?"

He laughed good-naturedly and said, "Not usually, but I'm strongly considering it."

"Well, I'll be over there if you need some help," I said and returned to my seat.

He actually did remarkably well for a rookie.

He pushed the baby carrier up until it rested in the crook of his arm and grasped the drink tray with that hand while pushing the stroller over to the condiment table with the other.

Once there he sat the drink tray down and creamed and sweetened the coffees while muttering, "I need another arm!"

When he was finished, he picked up the drink tray and backed toward the double doors pulling the stroller and balancing the drink tray.

Just before exiting, he caught my eye and hollered, "Piece of cake."

That was right before one of the twins escaped the stroller and ran across the store and out the other exit.

"Kristen!" he yelled, and then to me, "Me and my big mouth!"

I tracked the fugitive youngster with my eyes.

She ran around the outside, across the patio and came up behind him and with all the strength in her little two year-old body pulled the door open and held it for her daddy, grinning proudly all the while.

"That's my girl," he said, with obvious relief.

Once outside, Kristen jumped back into the stroller and they headed off to the parking lot where he would face yet another obstacle, i.e. how to get everyone back inside the van without dumping the drinks.

I was tempted to go and watch, but feared rousing the displeasure of Saint Arbuck who, as I had just witnessed, is also the patron saint of harried fathers.

2

I Haven't Been Myself

I haven't been myself lately.

I'm sure it has something to do with this weird transition we're in—residing in Las Vegas for four days a week and San Diego the other three.

Whatever the cause, it is really getting to me as witnessed by the following:

There we were earlier this morning...my beloved and I, at our usual table in our usual St. Arbuck's.

She, blazing through the Monday sudoku.

Me, contentedly sipping my coffee and not so contentedly reading of the Lakers' collapse in the second half of yesterday's playoff game versus the much hated, yet secretly admired Phoenix Suns.

To gain a more comfortable reading position, I crossed my legs.

I do that a lot.

Crossing my legs.

I don't know why.

Maybe it's a guy thing.

Anyway, as my eyes scanned down the newspaper column an

object appeared in the periphery of my vision that struck pure terror in my soul.

A slipper.

I saw a slipper.

Attached to my foot!

I glanced surreptitiously around our immediate area and said to my wife in a whisper, "Hey! I have slippers on."

She looked up from her calculations, spotted the humiliating footwear, and as a smile eased its way onto her quite lovely face said, "Why, yes you do."

"We have to go," said I.

"Why?"

"Why?" I repeated and then gestured silently at my feet.

She waved me off and said, "No one will even notice. Besides, all that means is that you are so comfortable at St. Arbuck's that coming here for you is just like walking into another room of the house."

I thought about that for a minute and concluded that while she was probably right, the fact remained that I, RG—a very manly man—was out in public wearing my slippers.

She glanced down at my feet, which were, by this time, tucked tightly up underneath my chair and said, "Well, at least you didn't wear the furry ones."

So I had that going for me.

Which was nice.

3

An Enchanted Moment

I don't like change.
If you want to know the truth, I somewhat despise it.
Ask my wife, she will gladly tell you all about it.
Anyway, I was sitting in my St. Arbuck's.
You know, THE St. Arbuck's.
The original.
I mean, Saint-freaking-Arbuck's!
The one currently being...remodeled.
No wonder people turn to drugs!
My table is gone—the one in the corner from which vantage point I have seen so much—replaced by a ten-foot long padded and upholstered high-backed bench with four tables and facing chairs.

I stood staring in disbelief realizing that my OCD is far more pronounced than I ever imagined.

Realizing that I really needed to move out of the way and let people have access to the condiment table, I sat in the middle.

To my surprise, I actually kind of liked it.

To my left I noticed a young fella in his early twenties.

To my right a young woman of the same age.

Both attractive in that funky, collegiate way, and both pecking away busily at notebook computers and stealing looks at each other around my frame—a frame that is twenty-five pounds lighter than one year ago, thank-you very much.

I looked at him, then at her, and realized that anything could happen...and probably would.

I leaned back a little, hoping that by doing so it would provide an opportunity for better eye contact between the two.

I waited.

And waited.

I drank some coffee and waited some more.

Nothing!

Every time she looked up, he was looking away, and vice-versa.

At one point, he stared at her for a full ten seconds while a group of five or six middle-school girls who were talking noisily outside on the patio captured her attention, but as soon as she turned to look at him, he looked down.

This went on for at least twenty-five minutes.

I cleared my throat loudly hoping that by doing so they would both look in my direction and perhaps catch each other's gaze.

Neither one budged.

Finally, with one last, lingering look his way, the young woman slowly and deliberately packed up her computer, books and Blackberry and stood to go.

While she walked over to the trash receptacle, he watched—obviously admiring her quite shapely form—but as soon as she turned to gather her belongings something on his computer screen was suddenly and irresistibly fascinating to him.

With undisguised frustration, she left the store and I could swear I heard Val Kilmer's voice (as Doc Holladay in the movie, *Tombstone*) saying, *"And she walked out of their lives forever."*

As the young man watched her go, his hand rose almost as if

of its own accord in a half-hearted wave and his mouth formed words that had somehow managed to bypass his vocal cords.

"Don't go," he finally said under his breath and then turned to me, eyes swimming with regret.

I hesitated and then said, "Stay there," as I raced out the door, to do what, well, I really didn't know.

I found her standing with one foot on the patio and the other on the pavement of the parking lot, seemingly paralyzed by indecision.

I approached slowly, hesitantly.

I mean after all, we *were* strangers.

She turned toward me, recognition registering in her eyes.

Suddenly feeling incomprehensibly shy and embarrassed I shoved both hands into the pockets of my cargo shorts and grinned.

She started to speak, but expelled a short breath of air, raised both arms out to the side and let them fall, slapping against her thighs as if to say, "What do I have to do to get this guy's attention? I mean, I'm cute, I'm here, and I'm available!"

I pressed my lips together into a tight smile and simply inclined my head in the direction of the entrance as if to say, "You should go back."

Her gaze flicked toward the entrance and then back to me and she raised her eyebrows quizzically.

I nodded a curt affirmation and without hesitation, she walked hurriedly toward the store and entered never breaking stride.

Through the window I saw her walk right up to him, hold out her hand for a handshake and mouth something that I could only surmise was her name.

A look of startled pleasure warmed his angular, handsome face and brushing aside long locks he shook her hand and invited her to sit beside him, which she did.

I watched for a few minutes as they laughed and chatted,

and when I returned to gather up my things...neither was even aware of my presence.

An enchanted moment.

4

The Big Spender

HE was just a little guy.

Standing there in line between two extremely tall men, he looked terribly tiny and lost.

He wore jeans, bright red athletic shoes, a Los Angeles Lakers sweatshirt and a baseball hat turned around backwards.

He kept leaning around the tall, tall man in front of him as if checking on how much longer he would have to wait.

I sat a few feet away observing the scene, and at one point, his bright, inquisitive eyes found mine.

Raising his eyebrows as if in amazement, he smiled and held up a twenty-dollar bill for me to see.

I whistled and returned his smile giving him a thumbs-up in the process.

When he finally reached the front of the line, his eyes barely cleared the counter.

In fact, the two baristas working the registers didn't see him for the longest time and kept calling other customers ahead of him.

He turned a hurt and fearful gaze toward his father who sat a short distance away at a table along the window.

The dad nodded his encouragement and the little guy turned as if to make one more attempt at ordering.

It was a big day.

It was the day he'd been waiting for a long time.

The day when he would get to order the very manly drinks by himself.

With twenty dollars.

His twenty dollars.

Evidently earned by himself through the labor of his hands and here he was in position to do just that, but the two young ladies towering above his head didn't even notice him.

His lip began to tremble ever so slightly and he looked once more toward his father for assistance.

As before, the dad smiled and nodded his encouragement.

The boy stretched his arms straight out from his side and let them fall, slapping against his thighs as if to say, "I'm not having any luck here, dad. What should I do now?"

A kindly soul who was next in line noticed the young lad's dilemma and said, "Ladies, I think you've got a paying customer down here," as he pointed to the boy.

One of the baristas leaned way over the counter and said, "Well, hello there, I didn't see you. Would you like something to drink?"

With a grin that threatened to split his face open, he said in a very clear, grown-up voice, "One small coffee and one small decraff...decanated..." his brow screwed up in puzzlement and he turned to his father one last time for support.

"Decaffeinated," his father said loudly with a smile.

"Yeah...what my dad said."

"All right," said the barista. "And what is your name?"

"Andy," said he.

"All right, Andy I'll get that right up for you."

I've never seen someone more eager to part with money except perhaps in the instance of going shopping with my daughter when she was still in high school and spending my money.

The barista brought the coffees back and sat them on the counter, being careful to warn the young man that the cups were extremely hot.

"In fact," she said, "I'm going to double-cup those coffees *and* put sleeves on them."

I'm not sure if he had the slightest idea of what she was talking about, but after paying for the drinks and returning his change very carefully to his front pocket, he accepted the drinks into his hands as if they were a treasure of great price.

"Come again, sweetie," said the smiling barista as he walked cautiously toward his dad.

And for the next half hour he sat there with his dad drinking a manly brew and talking about manly things, making an occasional face when taking in a mouthful of the strange tasting liquid.

It made me recall younger days when, under my uncle's tutelage I learned how to properly prepare and consume a cup of coffee.

Of course, no lesson in coffee consumption would have been complete without my uncle repeating one of his favorite coffee-time jokes which said, "Did you hear about the guy who went blind drinking coffee with sugar and cream?"

To which the other men would reply somewhat seriously, "No. How did that happen?"

And with scarcely concealed relish, my uncle would deliver the punch line.

"He forgot to take the spoon out."

I didn't get that joke until I was well into my high school years.

Of course, I always dutifully laughed right on cue because I was a boy among men and the men were laughing as if it was the funniest thing they'd ever heard.

Gazing fondly at the big spender and his dad, I had such a melancholy ache in my soul and at first, I couldn't figure out why.

Then I put it together.

My uncle was the most important man in my life.

Someone I loved.

Someone who was more of a dad to me than many biological fathers are to their sons.

I saw myself in that little boy, and I saw my uncle in that loving father.

On my way out, I stopped and said to that young father, "You're doing a good thing here, sir."

He grinned and said sincerely, "Why, thank-you. I learned it from my dad."

I bid them both a farewell and continued on my way.

As I climbed into my car, I recalled hearing someone say recently, "When a person is facing their last hours on earth, you never hear them complain about wishing they'd spent more time at the office."

Nor will you ever hear them say, "When my son was little I spent way too much time with him."

Driving out of the parking lot, I held my cell phone to my ear just in time to hear my uncle's raspy voice saying hello in his easy-going way.

"How are you doing?" I asked.

"Oh, I'm doing pretty good," came his typically buoyant reply.

Me too, uncle.

5

The Ring

S HE came slowly, almost shyly into view.

Halting of step, seemingly unsure of her direction.

"Dowdy" would have been my mother's appraisal of the poor soul.

The description fit, along with drab, dreary and dull.

Judging by her deeply lined face, she was definitely in the "golden years" of life.

Except, the look in her eyes bespoke a life that was anything but golden.

There was pain.

And behind the pain, fear.

And beyond that, just on the periphery as if readying for a full-fledged assault, there hung a cold front of despair.

It was a busy day for the cluster of restaurants at the Marketplace and I sat with uncommon ease on the patio of St. Arbuck's enjoying a cooling breeze along with my medium coffee, with room for cream.

St. Arbuck's had a queue stretching out the door.

I watched as she struggled to get a place in line a few feet away from me, only to be shoved rudely aside by three arrogantly aggressive teenaged girls.

Apparently dissatisfied with merely cutting in line the teens began to tease the poor woman about her outdated clothing.

"Oh, look," said one.

"Where'd you buy that, I'd like to get one?" taunted the blonde in the trio.

Unbelievably the woman was oblivious to the girl's insult.

Her eyes lit up as she started to reply, "Oh, I got it at—"

"Oh, my gosh!" said one of the others while rolling her eyes dramatically. "Don't you get it, you stupid old bag? It was a joke—you're the joke!"

The hurt couldn't have been more profound than if they would've just slapped her across her furrowed face.

"Oh," she mumbled quietly, dropping her gaze. "Oh, I see."

"Oh, I see," they mocked her reply, laughing raucously.

I'd had quite enough of their ill-mannered, emotional brutality and was half-way out of my seat when out of the corner of my eye I saw a tall, well-dressed young man rise to his feet and walk quickly toward the old woman.

He put his arm around her bony shoulders, gave her a sincere hug and said in a deep, Aussie brogue, "Grandmother, you're late. I've been worried about you."

She looked up at this kind stranger, confusion swimming in her eyes.

Then, all at once, she seemed to get it.

"Well," she said, playing along. "The traffic was a little worse than I expected."

The three teens looked on in silence, obviously intimidated by the newcomer.

The young man was fiercely handsome—someone who I am sure was quite attractive to the callous trio as was evidenced by their gape-mouthed stares.

He said as if noticing the three teens for the first time, "Oh,

I didn't notice you three. Is there something I can help you with?"

They shook their heads in a collective, "No," and turned around, standing in embarrassed silence.

After a minute or so, they kind of hurried off in a tight cluster, never looking back.

Watching them scurry away the old woman said, "That was, well, odd."

He smiled.

"Incredibly rude and mean-spirited would be a more apt description."

She returned the smile.

"Whatever the case, I thank you, young man, for coming to my rescue. It was very kind."

"Oh, no worries," said he. "No worries at all."

With a final hug, he was off to rejoin his companion—a striking blonde who looked as if she could be somebody famous.

By now the line had diminished somewhat and the old woman was standing right by my table.

I caught her eye, smiling my most winning smile.

She smiled back, albeit a bit warily.

"He beat me by about two seconds," I said, nodding in the direction of her champion.

She sighed deeply, shaking her head.

"I'm just an old woman, but I don't understand young people today."

"And who does?" came my rhetorical reply. "Fortunately most kids aren't like that bunch."

I glanced down at her left hand—she wore a diamond ring that had to be at the very least four carats.

Juxtaposed as it was to her attire, I found it to be extremely puzzling.

Her eyes followed my gaze.

"Charlie died one year ago today," she said sadly, randomly. "This is the first time I've been out." Indicating her dress she continued, "I just threw this old thing on; it was the first thing I came across in my closet."

The statement dripped with unspeakable sorrow especially in light of the selfish disregard the devilish trio had displayed toward one already wounded so deeply.

"According to my wife," said I, "she has an entire closet filled with dresses just like yours."

That brought a smile.

Suddenly I found myself saying impulsively, "Would you care to join me?"

Hesitating only slightly, she nodded a weary acceptance.

Once seated she said, "Now, I don't want to be an imposition."

"Don't even think about it," I said. "My wife will be along soon, so why don't you let me get you something to drink?"

Her initial protest notwithstanding, I did just that.

When my beloved finally arrived, we talked for a solid hour with that brave, sorrowing woman.

Throughout our meandering conversation, I couldn't shake the notion that while the circumstances that generated our encounter were not to my liking, I liked our new friend just fine.

I suppose you could write the whole thing off to chance.

Me?

I like to think of it like this: that young fella and I fulfilled some kind of assignment.

Sometimes random intersections aren't so random.

*In memory of Melba

6

Belle Of The Patio

SATURDAY morning at St. Arbuck's.

There he sat content in the supremacy that came from being the only dog on the patio.

Buster was his name.

French bulldog was his heritage.

And make no mistake, he was cute.

Such a face.

He looks exactly like the dog on the lid of the old Buster Brown shoe polish cans.

His owners, a young couple obviously proud of their pet sat drinking their beverages of choice and reading the morning paper.

I observed several people pausing to pet Buster and comment to the couple on his evident cuteness.

It was a moment to cherish.

That was all about to change.

My wife and I walked up with our pointy-eared, currently scruffy-faced, wonder dog, Trixie Belle—actually Ellie's Trixie Belle of the Ball to be precise—a 10 lb., jet black Miniature Schnauzer of some renown.

Suddenly the eyes of all were immediately drawn to her commanding presence.

Honesty compels me to mention that the very first ones to acknowledge her superiority were Buster's owners.

The woman even left her seat to squat in obeisance and attend to Trixie's scratching and nuzzling needs.

She said, "Oh, HE looks just like that dog in 101 Dalmatians... you know, the Scotty?"

I said, "SHE's a Miniature Schnauzer," a revelation which went completely over her head so enamored was she of Trixie.

It was a pitiable display of dog envy, and yet I had mercy on the poor woman and allowed her a full five minutes of Trixie's attention.

When Trixie was finished with her, she moved on to the man who, although stalwart in his initial resistance, eventually succumbed to her animal magnetism.

During this time Buster sat unnoticed and pouting under the table.

Feeling sorry for him—for as mentioned he is unarguably cute—I scratched his ears, for which he seemed to be grateful.

Having conquered that table Trixie moved on to others and before long was the center of attention.

Of course, for my wife and I this is such a common occurrence that we sat calmly and enjoyed our coffee/tangerine frappacino drinking and paper reading while the other guests kept Trixie occupied.

Buster and his people soon left as it was painfully obvious that he had lost the battle for patio dominance.

But he'll be back, as will others.

All for naught.

For Trixie is not only the "Belle of the ball," she is also conclusively Belle of the patio.

7

Conversations With Eddie-Part 1

EDDIE and I sat in the crowded interior of St. Arbuck's discussing our mutual discontent of all things Vegas.

Eddie Washington is a close friend who has been through a lot with me.

That's how you distinguish good friends from close friends, you know.

Close friends are the ones who after having seen you at your best and at your worst remain steadfastly loyal.

I'm not sure how many of those you get to have over the course of a lifetime.

Eddie is a disgustingly good-looking African-American man about 6'2" with shoulder length dreadlocks and pale green eyes which are startling against his café au lait complexion.

Did I mention that he's blessed with a naturally lean and muscular frame?

To compensate for his obvious physical handicaps, he's one of the best jazz drummers I know.

St. Arbuck's is nothing if not a place to just sit and engage in pleasant conversation with good friends.

Eddie and I have spent many hours doing just that.

"You know," Eddie said absently while watching a young mother trying unsuccessfully to herd a gaggle of toddlers out the door while at the same time clutching a wallet, coffee cup and yowling infant in her arms. "I really hate Las Vegas."

"Yeah," I replied, "but it's a dry hate."

He smiled at my old joke and sprang to the young woman's aid, holding the door open and suggesting lightheartedly that a second pair of arms might be beneficial.

She stared at him, frowning as if he'd spoken in a foreign tongue and hurried past without thanks or reply.

Once she was out the door, he returned to his seat, shaking his head in perplexity.

"Now see, that right there is what I'm talking about."

"What, just because she didn't fawn all over you in the manner to which you've become accustomed?"

"Nah, man! People are just mean spirited toward one another!"

"It's the heat," I said decisively. "How can you expect civility when it gets as hot as it does here?"

"It's not hot now. Last time I looked it was still hitting the thirties at night."

I said, "Yeah, but it's *going* to be hot and everyone knows it."

"That may be, but I'm civil! You're civil! What's the matter with the rest of these clowns?"

He had apparently spoken a little too loudly, for a thirty-something young man at the next table, whose face and eyes bore all the telltale signs of insufferable stress, looked up from a spreadsheet and said, "Excuse me, but I am *not* a clown!"

Eddie pierced the unfortunate fellow with a baleful gaze.

"Not talking to you, youngster. You just go on about your business."

The guy opened his mouth to speak, checked out Eddie's size and thought better of it; silently mouthed an overused, "Whatever!" and went back to his work.

"I see what you mean," said I, as the sarcasm dripped and formed a veritable puddle around the table's legs. "Civility is definitely one of your strong points."

He screwed up his face and said, "Ouch."

I said, "Your argument is not without merit, however. In fact, I find civility in decidedly short supply along with manners and common sense."

"Manners?" he said somewhat incredulously. "Can't remember the last time I saw any of those." After a brief pause he added, "Hard to blame that on the heat, though."

"I heard somebody say once that people are kind of like tea bags."

"Yeah? How's that?"

"Drop them in hot water and you'll get to see what comes out."

He was thoughtful for a few seconds.

"So, heat or no heat, what we're seein' is how people really are, they just keep it hid most of the time?"

"Dreadful sentence structure, but, yes."

A silver-haired elder approached the condiment table, limping painfully from a recent foot surgery.

As he passed by our table he turned and said, "Morning, boys. Isn't it a beautiful day to be alive?"

Eddie and I raised our cups and toasted him while giving voice to the fact that it indeed was a beautiful day to be alive.

8

Conversations With Eddie-Part 2

RECENTLY Eddie and I went on a road trip to Newport Beach.

Why?

Listen, going to Newport Beach does not require a reason... okay?

Anyway...

In a cost saving measure, we decided to share a room.

Two double beds.

Not a good idea.

Not a good idea at all.

Because, well, because he, uh, snores.

I mean I do too, but in Eddie's case we're talkin' the big leagues of snoring.

Prehistoric-dinosaur-in-the-throes-of-death snoring.

One might even say he was a bront-a-snorus.

(Sorry...I had to go for it.)

Snorr-est Whitaker.

(Okay, I'll stop.)

We went out for our nightly St. Arbuck's fix and then back to the room with the idea in mind of retiring early because we had a lot to accomplish the following day.

And, besides that, I was really tired from several nights of insomnia.

Don't ask.

So, the lights go out.

Eddie says, "Think you can go to sleep?"

"Yeah," I said, "as long as someone doesn't keep me awake."

"Oh, I'm not planning on talking."

"That's not what I mean."

He sat up and turned on the light.

"Oh? And just what do you mean?"

I turned to face him and said, "Dude, do I have to spell it out for you?"

He thought for a minute and then said, "You implying that I snore?"

I laughed.

"No, I'm not implying it, I'm flat out saying it."

His face arranged itself into a familiar pout.

"You just bein' mean spirited now."

And with that, he turned out the light, laid his head on the pillow and within five minutes was snoring with great vigor.

I reached for my shaving kit, inside of which I keep ear plugs, and to my horror...they weren't there.

Panic stitched a pattern across my sleep-starved consciousness.

What was I going to do?

I knew.

The gift shop in the hotel lobby.

It was my only hope.

I threw on a combination of clothes one would never want to be seen wearing in public.

I didn't care.

Down the elevator into the lobby where I was greeted by the oh-so-cheerful Asian night clerk.

I said, "Do you have any ear plugs?"

To which he replied with much smiling and head nodding.

Then he just stood there.

I repeated my question this time with a pronounced and dramatic snore.

Immediately his face brightened and he said something like, "Ahhhhhh."

With that he walked over to a rack of pamphlets where he selected one for the San Diego Zoo—one which featured a picture of elephants.

By then I realized I wasn't going to get anywhere with my happy host, so I simply said, "Thank-you," and went back to the room where I fantasized killing my feloniously resonating roommate.

I knew that it wasn't really an option—at least not yet—so I secured some toilet paper from the bathroom and proceeded to cram it tightly into my ears.

It did no good whatsoever!

My mind strayed to my original idea of murder.

I mean, who would blame me.

I could just see the investigating officers coming onto the scene.

I am cuffed and led downstairs into the lobby while the crime scene technicians examine the room.

Just as the arresting officer is ushering me out to a waiting squad car a stern-faced Detective Sergeant stops me, looks at my ears and says, "Oh, for cryin' out loud, Barney. Look at his ears... there's toilet paper stuffed in there. The vic was a snorer. Let him go, the bum deserved what he got."

I woke up to a sonorous serenade and our neighbor in the

room next door pounding out his complaint on the adjoining wall. Maybe I could actually get away with it...

Film at eleven.

9

Thirty Second
Relationships

HOW are you doing? she asked, her perpetual smile firmly affixed.

I gave my stock reply, "I'm doing better than I deserve."

"You always say that," she said, filling a 16 oz. cup with the coffee of the day.

"Well, it's really how I feel."

She sat the medium coffee, with room for cream, on the counter and rang it up.

"One eighty-one," she said accepting my money. "I don't know. I feel like I deserve a lot more than I have." After a pause she continued, "He was out all night again."

"He" was her live-in boyfriend.

"What was it this time?" I asked.

As she counted out my change she said, "He said he just needed some time with his buddies. Funny thing, though...I didn't realize any of his buddies used 'Happy' as a fragrance of choice."

"So, he's seeing someone else?"

"Gee, you think?"

Total elapsed time: thirty seconds.

Her name is Rachel.

Her official title is, barista.

I see her most mornings at my favorite St. Arbuck's.

She always greets me with a ready smile, which I know hides a lot of pain.

Hovering perilously close to forty, she doesn't like the person she's become.

Her ex-husband abandoned her two years previously to go in search of a "soul-mate."

The pain of rejection is still quite intense.

She now lives with a man who is not her husband.

He hasn't held a full-time job in over five years and, if he were to be completely honest, doesn't really see the need to look for one.

Most of the time he treats her badly.

As a young woman she had intended to get a degree in education in hopes of fulfilling a lifelong dream to teach kindergarten.

The closest she got was one year when she and her "ex" lived across the street from a community college.

Her hair is too thin and her waist too thick.

Her stomach is delicate and her hands are manly, or so she's been told.

She has a drug problem.

At least she's honest about it.

She's considered visiting a twelve-step group, but as yet hasn't made the effort to go.

Maybe next week..

Her feet hurt all the time and she fears that her back is starting to go from all the time spent standing in one spot and taking orders.

No one would ever consider Rachel to be attractive, but that's only because they can't see her heart.

Behind it all—all the hurt, all the failed expectations—there beats the heart of a dreamer; a passionate lover of good books and good movies; a loyalist; a giver of whatever she has that you may need.

She fears that her future is already upon her, and that this is it...a thirty-hour a week job with irregular hours.

She fears that she has already grown so complacent that she will never try to find a pathway to something more.

And yet, she hopes.

All of this I learned over a period of two years in a series of conversations lasting an average of thirty seconds.

I feel like I know this woman, which is good, because she is worth knowing.

And when I hear various individuals talking about how tight their schedules are and how they just don't have time to get to know anyone, I want to tell them Rachel's story.

She's not the only one.

There are many thirty second relationships in my world.

Thirty seconds invested five days per week works out to about two minutes and thirty seconds of invested time.

Two minutes and thirty seconds per week works out to around ten minutes a month, which would then translate into two hours per year.

Trust me, it's worth the investment.

10

Love You Forever

MY wife and I were doing our usual thing at St. Arbuck's—she conquering yet another sudoku puzzle and me reading through the sports section while enjoying our beverages of choice.

A young mother and her son entered and sat at the table right in front of us.

The name emblazoned in a nearly illegible scrawl on her cup of coffee said, "Veronica."

If I had to guess their ages, I would say that Veronica was around thirty and the boy perhaps two and a half.

She took great care in placing her son in a seat next to her, fussing over him so as to insure not only his comfort but also his safety.

When he was well-settled, she opened a bottle of chocolate milk which he accepted gleefully and began to drink.

He was a bit too eager and predictably, an entire mouthful of the silky sweet liquid escaped and cascaded down his chin soaking his very stylish shirt.

He looked down at the mess and began to cry.

Veronica immediately picked him up and sat him on her

lap giving comfort that only loving mothers can provide in such moments.

He calmed down and had another go at the chocolate milk making sure this time that the sips were manageable.

She sat with her arms around him and her head resting on top of his brown wavy locks, eyes closed, lost in a moment of maternal bliss that was nearly rapturous in its appearance.

For in that moment no one else on earth existed except her and that beloved child.

The insistent ring of her cell phone shattered the scene.

And while I could only hear one side of the conversation, what transpired was heartbreaking.

After the initial small-talk, her face took on a sad, wounded look and she said, "Yes, well, I'm not sure you really want to hear about that."

Apparently, the caller did and she reluctantly continued, "Well, it's not good. Yesterday my attorney called and said that David is going to ask for full custody. Can you believe it? He said David intends to claim that I'm an unfit mother..."

It was here that her voice broke and her grip on the child tightened unconsciously.

After a few seconds of silence during which time she listened to her caller's remarks she said, "I know all that, but this means that I'm going to have to go in there and defend myself like I've done something wrong."

By this time, the tears were flowing liberally.

The child looked at his mommy and with a tiny hand reached up and gently brushed away her tears and laid his head against her breast.

The love exchanged between these two was nearly tangible in its intensity.

My wife and I glanced at each other shaking our heads sadly.

Finally, Veronica said, "Well, I'd better be going. I'll call you later on...I love you, mom."

She closed the lid on her cell phone, returned it to her purse and choked back a sob that had risen unbidden in her throat.

The child turned on her lap so he was facing her and placing a hand on either side of her face said in his little boy voice, "Be awight, mommy."

She wrapped that precious child in her arms and covered his head and face with kisses, rocking him back and forth... back and forth bringing to mind a line from the Robert Munsch classic that my wife used to recite to our kids when they were little: *"I'll love you forever, I'll like you for always; as long as I'm living my baby you'll be."*

Love you forever.

Yes, she would.

11

About Birds And Stuff

THE patio of St. Arbuck's is crowded with people who, like me, seek to take advantage of the relative coolness of the morning.

Nine AM and only 80 degrees...not bad for June 6th in Las Vegas.

I haven't been to the gym for over a week.

I've actually decided that driving by and looking through the window is as good as working out.

Okay, it's just a theory at this point, but I'm working on it.

A blackbird hops aggressively toward six or seven sparrows that were competing over a scrap of pastry discarded by a careless patron.

Leaping into the middle of the boisterous gathering, he seeks to intimidate them into leaving, but they'll have none of it!

They form in a tightly clustered knot around the prize refusing to budge.

After much fluttering, puffing and shrieking the blackbird flees to a nearby mesquite tree where he lets the scrappy little fellows know exactly what he thinks of them collectively and individually.

Or so it seems to me.

In the melee, a young sparrow has managed to wedge himself in close to the scrap of food.

Dragging it out from the midst of the older warriors, he flies away with the thing jutting comically from his woefully insufficient beak.

His elders are completely unaware and conclude their verbal jousting with the blackbird raider by turning back to resume the challenge for the food.

It is, of course, gone and they stand in a loose circle looking at one another, looking around...looking at me as if to say, "What the heck?!"

Twenty feet away the youngster is having a feast.

They never see him.

It makes me smile.

12

Church Lady

SHE'S there every day.
Wing chair.
Over by the window.
Bird's-eye view of the front door.
A smallish woman of about seventy years, although you'd never know it to look at her, with stylishly cropped gray hair and clothes to match.

Funky, European-style glasses perch comfortably on her nose and with her ever-present scarf, she looks as if she could've just breezed in right off the streets of Barcelona.

Her face is lined, but every line tells a story.

Stories about refusing to allow challenging circumstances to dominate her life.

Stories about facing each challenge with grit and determination and refusing to fall prey to a victim mentality.

There has been sorrow.

Plenty of it.

But as she says frequently, "Weeping endures for a night, but joy comes in the morning."

She is particularly fond of passion tea, which suits her for she is a woman of amazing passion.

Her zest for life is infectious as evidenced by the nearly unbroken ranks of friends who drop by to chat just for a minute or two before hurrying on with their busy lives.

In those off moments when not otherwise occupied, she smiles at strangers and wishes them a good day, a greeting most often returned guardedly if returned at all.

But I've seen more than one skeptic won over by her enthusiastic persistence.

She is the type of person you just want to be around for it seems that she has "cracked the code" on how to approach each day as if it held great promise.

Sometimes I hear her make references to "church", but only in passing as if there has been a conscious decision on her part to live out her faith rather than just talk about it.

I somehow get the feeling that St. Arbuck's is her cathedral, for it is here in the midst of the hectic comings and goings of everyday life that she has found a grateful and dedicated congregation.

I asked her one time if she would be willing to reveal her secret to building relationships.

She replied without hesitation, "Authenticity. I ask people how they are doing, and then I sit back and listen to what they say with undivided attention."

Imagine that.

Can one person change the world?

Can the world really be won by one?

Somewhere in San Diego, the church lady is on a mission.

13

The Horror

IT was a pleasant, if coolish, mid-October morning on the Pacific Garden Mall in downtown Santa Cruz, California. My wife and I sat on the patio of a funky St. Arbuck's right across the street from the historic Palomar Inn.

Formerly the home of the Santa Cruz German Beer Gardens, St. Arbuck's now hosted a steady stream of university students, local business people and a smattering of surfers stopping in after an early morning session at Steamer Lane.

It was an extraordinary occasion for my wife as she was having her very first Mocha.

"Ecstatic" falls pitifully short of describing my emotional state, as this was a moment for which I had long hoped.

We were enjoying ourselves immensely, blissfully ignorant of the horror that was about to unfold. .

In hindsight, had we known then what we were about to behold I am certain we would have fled rather than be witness to the carnage.

We had just given a brief interview to two lovely young Asian university students when we heard the words that struck terror in our souls and sent a chain reaction of stunned disbelief rippling through the caffeine crazed patrons pouring in from the sidewalk.

"I'm sorry, but we are closed," the store manager said cautiously as she stood tentatively blocking access to the entryway.

A collective, "What?" was raised from six or seven patrons who were just walking up.

"Yeah, we're closed," she said with a nervous chuckle that did little to disguise the stark terror one could see in her eyes. "It's the plumbing...it's all backed up, and, well, it's not a good situation."

The people stared in stuporous silence unable to will their lips to utter a sound.

They looked at her; she looked at them; they looked at each other; some looked hungrily at the beverages my wife and I shamelessly hoisted to our lips.

Sensing an entrepreneurial opportunity I said, "I'll sell you a sip of my coffee for a buck."

While I thought the comment hilarious, no one else thought I was the least bit funny.

In fact, one fellow bared his teeth in a feral grimace that quickly made me abort further witticisms.

One well-dressed young woman, her otherwise beautiful eyes peering suspiciously beneath a wrinkled brow said, "You're seriously closed?"

"It'll only be for about an hour," said the harried manager hopefully.

The door opened just wide enough for a hand to thrust a stack of coupons her way before drawing back quickly.

Fixing a don't-kill-me-I'm-only-the-messenger smile on her face the manager said sheepishly, "So, here's a coupon for a free drink when you come back."

After a few more seconds of staring, the people sullenly accepted the bribe and stumbled off without uttering a word.

The manager turned her attention our way, sighed deeply and said, "This really stinks!"

We could only nod our agreement as a couple more people walked toward the entrance.

Their countenances, once bright with anticipation, fell pitifully upon hearing the awful news.

And so it went for the next fifteen minutes or so as we sat transfixed by the unfolding drama.

She said, "These people are my friends. I hate doing this to them!"

"Oh, I'm sure they'll survive," I said encouragingly.

Her eyes widened and she replied, "You don't know some of them. This is, like, their life. I mean you interrupt their routine and..."

The sentence hung there unfinished as three more patrons approached.

"Hi," she said with faux good cheer. "I'm sorry but we're closed for about an hour."

The three stopped dead in their tracks as if they had run into an invisible shield.

Finally, one whimpered, "Closed?"

It was pathetic!

I wanted to shout, "Yeah, closed. What part of that didn't you understand?" And yet I didn't, knowing full well that had I not escaped the circle of death, so to speak, I too would have been among the distraught, distressed, overwrought and downright horror-stricken.

She must've handed out two or three dozen free drink coupons prompting me to inquire, "So, what's to stop some enterprising domestically challenged (i.e. homeless) individual from rounding up a few buddies and availing themselves of the freebies?"

"Because," she said with a knowing wink, "I've worked here for three years and I know most of them."

Ultimately, it exacted a terrible toll causing her to surrender the position to a quite unwilling replacement while muttering, "I can't take this any longer," and fleeing for the relative safety of the store's interior where, apparently, the stench of raw sewage was preferable to the terrible sight of legions of shell-shocked regulars.

Actually, who could blame her?

14

Captain Mike

MY wife and I were at the Hartsfield-Jackson International Airport in Atlanta, Georgia waiting for a connecting flight back to Las Vegas.

With over an hour to kill, we decided the occasion merited a trip to the St. Arbuck's adjacent to the food court.

Spying a table away from the crush of travelers, we sat down to enjoy our brews, a medium coffee—with room for cream—for me, and a small mocha for her.

At the next table sat a pleasant looking young man wearing a tee shirt bearing a line across the front that read, "Real pilots don't need ejection seats," along with something about Anbar province in Iraq.

He was staring at some pictures arrayed on the table in front of him.

I said, "Are you going or coming?"

He looked up as if he hadn't understood the question and then said, "Oh, I'm on my way back for deployment. My third tour."

My wife pointed to the pictures and said, "Are those your children?"

His face brightened.

"Oh, yes ma'am." Scooting closer to our table, he handed the pictures to her, pointed to a cute little redheaded girl and continued, "That's Kylie—she just turned three last weekend. And that little guy," he tapped the picture of an infant, "is Corbin. He's six months."

I was watching his expression while he spoke. He seemed to be barely holding it together.

My wife said, "Do you have a picture of your wife?"

Digging quickly into his shoulder bag, he produced a laminated photograph of a pretty girl wearing a tank-top, shorts and a baseball cap with the slogan, "Will Fly For Food," emblazoned across the front.

"She's very pretty." Gesturing at his shirt I said, "Are you a pilot?"

"Yes, sir," he said. "I'm assigned to the Marine Light Attack Helicopter Squadron 775, Marine Aircraft Group 16, 3rd Marine Air Wing, Marine Corps Air Station Miramar."

I laughed.

"That's a mouthful."

"It is," he said joining my laughter. "It surely is."

"What is your job?"

"I fly the AH-1W Super Cobra. We do escort of transport helicopters and ground convoys, armed reconnaissance, helicopter air-to-air attack, anti-shipping operations, and coordination and terminal control of fixed wing Close Air Support, artillery, mortars, and naval gunfire."

"That's it?" I said jokingly.

As he laughed my wife said, "Are you an officer?"

"Sorry for not making a proper introduction earlier," he said apologetically. "Mike is the name and I'm a Captain," he said while extending his hand.

I introduced my wife and myself and said, "It's a pleasure to meet you, Captain," while we shook hands.

My wife said, "Are you on your way back to San Diego?"

"Yes, ma'am. I've been down in Augusta visiting my folks."

I said, "That would explain the accent."

"Oh, yes sir," he said proudly. "Southern born and raised."

My wife handed him the pictures and said, "When do you leave for Iraq?"

He was quiet for a few moments as if struggling to control his emotions.

"Ah, sorry. I don't know why, but this time is really hard. I mean they've all been hard, but this one especially so." Squaring his shoulders and sitting a little straighter he said, "Anyway, I leave in two days which gives me just enough time to get home, get my things squared away and say a proper goodbye to my wife and kids."

We didn't really know what to say after that and sat in an uncomfortable silence.

Finally, he said, "Can I tell you something?"

"Sure," I said glancing at my wife. "Anything."

"I don't know why I'm doing this, except for the fact that you seem like really nice folks and all, but I'm scared. No, more than scared, I'm terrified. Terrified that maybe this time I'm not going to dodge the bullet. That maybe this time...I won't be coming home; that I won't be around to see my kids grow up; that my wife..."

He couldn't finish the sentence as his emotions got the best of him.

After a bit my wife said, "You're about my son's age, and if it were my son sitting in that seat saying the things you're saying, I'd just give him a big hug." Pausing for a couple of seconds she said, "Can I give you a hug?"

He blinked rapidly trying to hold back the tears and said, "Oh, yes ma'am, you can. You surely can."

Leaning toward him, she hugged that tough Marine Captain and just held on to him while he cried a little.

As they both sat back in their chairs, Captain Mike looked decidedly embarrassed.

"Sorry about that," he said while wiping his eyes with the backs of his hands. "But I guess it's been coming for a while."

"Real men *do* cry," I said lightly.

Looking down at his shirt he added, "Yeah, real pilots too." Without fanfare, he stood, gathered his things and said, "Well, I've got a plane to catch."

I thought he was going to leave, but instead he looked each of us in the eye, snapped off a crisp salute and with his mouth in a thin, straight line, nodded his head once, then turned on his heels, and walked away toward a future that was uncertain at best.

"That was very cool," I said.

"What's that?"

"The salute. It's the highest honor a soldier can pay to someone."

My wife's mouth turned down at the corners and she dabbed at her eyes with a tissue. "I won't forget him," she said, her voice raw with emotion.

"No," I agreed, "no, we won't."

15

The Old Couple

THE old couple sat by the window—he, nearing eighty, she, looking back to see seventy.

It was early Sunday morning at St. Arbuck's and I was at my usual place in the corner.

There is something about busy people on the go that I find particularly inspiring.

Distracted by my surreptitious eavesdropping, however, this morning I accomplished little else.

There was something deeply compelling by this aged pair.

I learned right away that they weren't married but had only just met and decided to share a hot brew together.

They talked of their lives, of their lost loves—each had lost a partner to catastrophic illness.

They talked of the difficulties the aging process forces one to encounter.

The old gentleman said at one point, "I'll be honest with you—I haven't gone to a movie in twenty years."

Expressing shock she replied, "That's amazing! Why?"

"I just don't do well in large crowds," he said, his palsied hand quivering rhythmically as he lifted his coffee toward his lips.

"I know what you mean. When my husband was alive we were so in love that anywhere we went it seemed like we were the only ones in the room." Her voice choked with emotion. After a moment she added, "I'm sorry."

His eyes filled with tears, recalling, no doubt, similar experiences.

They sat like that for a moment, lost in memory.

Finally, they looked at each other, their eyes locking, and broke into laughter.

"Oh, we're a fine pair, we are," he said, slapping his bony thigh.

She sobered, nodded her head silently before saying, "It was good, wasn't it? You know, being with someone whose love was so strong you never had to worry."

His wrinkled face relaxed into a wistful smile. "Oh, you bet. You bet."

After a brief pause he smoothed the newspaper, scrutinized it as if searching for something in particular.

He glanced her way and then once again at the page.

"You know, I could probably be talked in to going to the movies."

She laughed and blew her nose on a tissue.

"Oh, you think so, do you?"

They talked for a while more about what they might see and where.

Me? I was lost in the wonder.

Provisional or providential I know not.

What I do know is that I had just been witness to something exceptional.

Something fine, good, and healing.

I wanted to rush home as quickly as possible and gather my lady into my arms, tell her that she's made my life worth living and that, to quote an old song, "She's the best thing that ever happened to me."

I want to sit with her some day, at St. Arbuck's, and have some young buck eavesdrop on our conversation and be, perhaps, encouraged to go and do the same.

I want to be with her the rest of my days.

And I will.

16

A Day In The Life

THE morning's misty, mysterious mantle of fog seemed to envelop me like the embrace of an old friend as I sat at my favorite beachside St. Arbuck's.

A couple of teenaged lovers sat as one in an overstuffed chair, heads resting on one another's shoulders and sound asleep, out of place amidst the harried and hurried throngs of customers.

The homeless man passed me on his way to use the restroom, bleary eyed and stumbling after a night of too much of everything, the vapor trail left in his wake strong enough to make my eyes smart.

A young man dressed in designer slacks, high thread count white cotton shirt and silk tie talked loudly on a "blue-tooth" while awaiting the completion of his order, oblivious to the volume with which he spoke.

Three aged mothers sat around a table across the patio bravely discussing their plans for next summer, but in their eyes I could see an onrushing cold front of doubt as to whether another summer would be seen.

The high school girl dressed in a skirt short enough to be nearly cheek-baring stood impatiently in line speaking discourteously to her mother whose gaze, cast briefly my way, seemed to beg, "What can I do?"

A female barista cleaned the condiment table; young, yet already bearing the weight of her years as evidenced by the stoop in her shoulders.

The Chocolate Lab barked loudly as he awaited the return of his pierced and tattooed mistress who had disappeared inside the women's restroom some ten minutes past...thinking, no doubt, that he had at last been abandoned as he always feared he would.

A sip of coffee and a sigh.

Just another day in the life.

17

Maggie

WHEN my son was little, he used to tell me I had "a way of dogs."

I'm not quite sure what meaning was ascribed to the phrase in his seven year-old mind, but I took it as a compliment.

Over the years, it kind of stuck to the point that it's become a family joke of sorts.

But it's not a joke...I love dogs.

Sometimes when I have nothing better to do, I will go to a random pet store and look at puppies, or go to the local rescue shelter and gaze at a few dozen sets of warm brown eyes and wish I had a country estate so I could take them all home.

I was at St. Arbuck's early today.

Mornings are good thinking time and good thinking generally produces good writing.

Generally.

Anyway...

My second favorite dog in the entire world came in with her master.

Her name is Maggie.

She's an English bulldog.

A licking, slobbering seventy-pound hunka-hunka burnin' love.

Tail wagging is for other less fortunate canines.

For Maggie, it's a full-body experience.

If she likes you, that is.

She likes me.

She'll sit calmly by her master's side, gazing through the window to see if anyone will pay her any attention.

I, of course, hold out for all of five seconds.

Then I exit the store, call her name and watch as she goes into her act.

First, there's the body wiggle, followed by a full-throated greeting, which is merely preparatory to that for which she most longs—to bestow a jolly good slobbering.

She really can't be content until the object of her affection has been good and slobbered.

The master carries an extra towel for just such an eventuality.

After having been satisfied that her subject has had enough, she dips her head and waits patiently.

For what, you ask?

Why, it's time for the scratching.

But not just any scratching.

Nooooooooooo.

Maggie tolerates nothing short of what amounts to deep tissue manipulation.

It's kind of like doggie shiatsu—head, ears, shoulders and finally tail stub.

She really likes the tail stub rub.

And who wouldn't?

Modesty prohibits me from...oh, what the heck...I am an expert in tail stub rubs.

Ask anyone.

Ask Maggie.

At some point—and the timing varies greatly—she will lose all motor control and just collapse onto the ground, her great pink tongue lolling out of the corner of her mouth as if she were road kill.

Then, and only then, is it safe to walk away.

Her master?

Oh, he's a nice guy.

But it's all about the dog.

It's always all about the dog.

Sadly, she's seven years old now.

Bulldogs don't live much past nine or ten.

For now, she's my little doggie buddy.

18

The Treasure

THAT is not what I meant!

The twenty-something guy at the next table talking on his Blackberry (i.e. "crack-berry" for those truly addicted) seemed to grow ever more distraught as the conversation progressed.

St. Arbuck's was unusually empty for a Thursday evening, but in OB anyway, most of the action was out on the street and was thus understandable.

"Why would I say something like that?"

While I couldn't be sure of the identity of the party on the other end of the line, my guess was a girlfriend or spouse.

"She said that? She really said that?"

His face reflected all the signs of stress: flushed, perspiring, eyes wide and blinking rapidly, mouth working even while listening.

"Listen, I don't know what else to say. It's just not true!"

This last statement was accompanied by a slap on the table top.

Glancing my way he rolled his eyes, holding one hand out to the side, palm up as if to say, "Can you believe this?"

"I'm coming over there right now." (Listening) "What do you mean I can't?" (Listening) "I live there."

He suddenly seemed to deflate as if all the air had gone out of him.

"Used to? I *used* to live there? What does that mean?"

He was a pathetic figure.

With one hand, he held the cell phone to his ear as if it were one end of a lifeline.

With the other, he cradled his head miserably.

"Baby, don't...don't...please don't say that."

By this time, his voice was cracking, and I heard him sniff as he appeared to brush away a tear.

Without another word, he sat the phone on the table and covered his face with both hands.

I didn't know what to do, or even if I should do anything at all, but he seemed so hopeless.

"It sounded as if that went well," I said lightly, sarcastically.

He looked up and snorted out a, "You have no idea."

"Wife?"

He nodded almost imperceptibly.

"Yep. Married three months."

I smiled and said, "You want to talk about it?"

Raising his arms and letting them fall heavily to his side he said, "She's decided that we made a horrible mistake—no, strike that, her *mother* has decided that we made a horrible mistake."

"That's some pretty tough opposition," I said. "Did you know about this going in, or is it a new revelation."

"Oh, I knew about it. I just thought we could, you know, fix it."

I said, "So, what are you going to do now?"

He shook his head sadly.

"I don't know...I just don't know."

"Can I make a suggestion? You know, comfort of strangers and all that."

He said, "Sure. Go for it."

"Do you love her?"

"I'm crazy in love with her."

"Does she love you?"

"I thought so...no, I'm sure of it."

I said, "Is her mother entirely to blame for your problems?"

"Well," he said a bit sheepishly, "I'm to blame for a fair amount."

"Do you dislike her mother?"

"Not really. I mean I'm a little put out with her right now, but she's a nice lady. She just doesn't get me."

I said, "Do you 'get' her?"

He was thoughtful for a few seconds and then said, "No...I can't say that I do."

"So, your wife has her mother on the one side—who she most likely is desperate to please—and you on the other, and is being torn apart by the conflict. That sound about right?"

He sighed, "Man, you just cut right to the heart, don't you?"

"Hey," I said, "it's just a thought." After a brief pause I continued, "What would happen if you called her mother and offered to get together and work this out? Tell her she's a good woman and that she raised a good girl. It's like I heard someone say once—if you speak to the treasure it will rise up."

"She'd drop dead of a heart attack!" he said with a laugh, and then, "You're serious, aren't you?"

"Like I said, it's a thought."

"Speak to the treasure, huh?" He stood suddenly. "Well, if I'm going to do this, I just have to go do it or else I'll chicken out."

"Good luck," I said with a smile.

He started to leave and then turned back.

"Hey," he said while shaking my hand. "Thanks. Maybe I'll run into you again."

"Maybe," I said as he walked out into the night.

Just before the door closed behind him I heard him mutter, "Speak to the treasure. It just might work."

19

Public In-Convenience

I am of the opinion that public places, St. Arbuck's included, should all come equipped with public conveniences (read "restrooms").

Make that TWO restrooms—one for each gender.

So there I was, working happily away at my writing, when nature called.

The first challenge was whether to leave my laptop on the table top while I answered said call.

I scanned the room for possible criminal types.

Apart from a local politician, I found none and therefore felt safe to leave it and the rest of my belongings behind.

This particular store has a "unisex" restroom.

For the unenlightened among you, the term means that the facility is open to one and all regardless of race, creed or gender.

Not wishing to alarm anyone inside who may be currently enjoying the use of the space, I jiggled the door handle lightly.

The door opened.

I entered and, well, sat down to do my, uh, you know... business.

At mid-point as my eyes were roving aimlessly around the small enclosure they happened to light upon the inner door handle whereupon I made a horrifying discovery: I had forgotten to lock the door.

As you can imagine this generated an immediate quandary and no small amount of angst.

Should I pause from doing my business and correct the mistake, or should I hurry things along in hopes that I can conclude before another patron barged in.

I chose the latter.

Successfully, I might add.

After washing up, I opened the door only to come face to face with one of the female baristas.

We stood there in an awkward silence.

She looked past me into the room.

I found her eyes and gave my head a little shake as if to say, "You don't want to go in there."

With wrinkled brow, she thought about it for a few seconds before giving me a small smile, nodding knowingly and returning to her work.

Me, I slunk back to my table, packed up my stuff and left, embarrassment clinging to me like a death shroud.

The moral of this story is this: when in a "unisex" restroom... do yourself a favor and make sure to lock the door behind you.

20

Happy Feet

ON this late fall morning, my normal focus seems a bit askew.

I am forstraught, and fistulous.

Yeah, I don't know what it means either, but it sounds really good.

My brain seems encased in stone.

Distractions abound.

Basically, I have writer's block!!

"And pray thee, R.G., what would be the reason for this uncommonly hateful occurrence?"

So good of you to inquire.

That would be the collection of drivel I jokingly refer to in more sane moments as my fifth novel!

The contemptible brute is stuck at page 157 and no amount of pleading, cajoling or threatening of my muse seems to produce the slightest bit of creativity.

Forsaken and floundering I stare stupidly at the busy people who enter and leave St. Arbuck's in a nearly unbroken thread.

My fingers drum absently on the table, no doubt an auditory irritant to the real estate broker seated a mere three feet away.

Without warning, happy feet overtake me.

From the knees down, there's a party going on.

Looking down at the silly appendages, I will them to stop.

I am ignored.

I stomp one foot on top of the other.

In rebellious response, the frenzy increases.

Snatching at a desperate remedy, I attempt to cross my legs and in the process, I destroy my right kneecap on an exposed screw head on the stout table's underside.

While I grasp and gasp, the left foot taps out a crazy rhythm that, incredibly, is joined by my right foot in complete and utter disdain of my suffering.

Am I not master of my own body?

Apparently not, as the revelry intensifies.

I stomp both feet on the floor.

They take it as a signal for more frivolity.

My carrying on attracts the attention of a barista on his cleaning rounds.

A fellow "Muso," we've become friends over a period of time and talk music frequently.

"Are you all right?" he says while mopping up spillage from some careless customer.

I point to my crazily dancing feet.

"Does this look like I'm all right?"

Nodding in solemn understanding he says, "Happy feet?"

"I can't get them to stop!" is my desperate reply.

"Hmmm," says he walking slowly over for a closer look.

Bending low he examines my extremities making those "Tsk, tsk," noises that doctors always make right before they give you the bad news.

"What?"

Standing upright he lays a gentle hand on my shoulder.

"I'm afraid I've got bad news."

My feet danced on.

"Bad news?"

Walking in a slow circle around the table he says, "You have a very serious condition."

"Serious condition?"

I have this bad habit of repeating everything a bearer of bad news says and this morning I was in fine fettle.

He pulled up a chair and sat.

"Very serious."

I wait a full ten seconds in silence before saying, "Well?"

"You have a bad case of what we in the industry call the boogie-woogie flu."

Dear Lord, not that!

"And," he continued, "there is only one known cure."

"Which is...?" I prompted.

He glanced around as if making sure we wouldn't be overheard.

"Well, there's no way to break this to you gently, so let me just go ahead and say it. Brace yourself."

I braced for the worst.

"Okay...let me have it."

"You have to listen to two hours of Elvis every day for seven days."

I could feel the blood drain from my face as the room began a topsy-turvy tilt.

"And..." he said.

"Good grief, man! You mean there's more??!!"

"Oh yes, in addition to that you must learn and perform a spirited, heart-felt rendition of *Hound Dog* at a Karaoke club."

I sat in stunned silence too numb to reply.

"Sorry bro."

With that, he stood and returned to his work.

I look down at my happy feet, wondering which was worse—the malady or the cure.

After about five seconds thought, I chose the malady.

I mean, come on, there are some things a man just can't do and live with himself.

21

Customer Service

S T. Arbuck's was at its best.

People gathered around tables, engaged in the comfortable camaraderie that comes with just being together and enjoying good conversation.

There seems to have been a lot of talk lately about how St. Arbuck's has lost some of its "soul."

I beg to differ.

To judge the soul of St. Arbuck's merely on the basis of its baristas' performance or what it smells like when you first enter, or even how one's espresso is drawn is to miss part of the picture.

The "soul" in question has at least as much to do with the people who crowd through the doorways morning after morning—as well as those who drop in to while away a pleasant afternoon or evening—as corporate policy and practices.

Case in point.

One recent morning I sat in my St. Arbuck's enjoying my usual, a medium coffee with room for cream, and struggling through a quite poorly written paragraph in which a sportswriter detailed several compelling reasons as to why the Lakers were going to be swept in the playoffs.

Again.

Funny, I thought it was a "newspaper."

The Lakers getting swept, at least in this decade, isn't exactly news.

Where was I?

Oh yes...

So, there I was quietly reading and sipping when all of a sudden I heard angry voices.

To be fair, it was only one voice.

One loud and angry *male* voice to be exact.

So disruptive was the individual's tirade that I finally left my seat to go investigate.

Behind the coffee bar, three baristas—two women and one man—stood in mute silence as the angry vulgarian lambasted them jointly and severally for getting his order wrong.

"But sir," said the shift leader, "it's exactly what you told us. Look on the side of the cup. We repeat your order before we write it down. We repeated it, and you confirmed it."

He lashed out with an angry reply.

"I'm just about sick of your attitude and arrogance! When I get through with you people you'll be working someplace else... that is if you are working at all!"

By this time the other customers, both those in line and those seated at tables, had ceased conversing and all eyes were trained on the situation, for that is exactly what it had become—a situation.

The shift manager was in a tough position.

She had to pacify an individual—who I judged to be either off his meds or just plain nasty—while at the same time keeping the other customers moving through the line.

"Sir, if you'll just step over here we'll remake your drink and let these other folks place their orders."

"No I won't step over there!" he bellowed. "You think I care two cents about these clowns in line?"

Smiling sweetly she replied, "Actually, I'm quite sure you don't, but you really need to step out of line and let the others order."

He tossed a disdainful glare toward the long line of customers, most of whom appeared to be ready to take matters into their own hands.

The shift manager stepped out from behind the counter, still smiling, and said, "How about if I give you a five dollar gift card for your trouble?"

He was having none of it.

"Oh, so that's how you're going to play it. First, you get my drink order wrong and now you're going to try to buy me off. I don't think so!"

By then I had worked my way to where I was right behind the brute, as had a couple of other regulars.

Somebody in line hollered, "Take the card and get going, moron!"

A chorus of agreement arose which only seemed to solidify the man's resolve to fight to the bitter end, which, by my estimation was just seconds away if he didn't change his approach.

Then, in defiance of all reasoned logic, the man's shoulders slumped, his hands flew to his face and he began to sob.

We're talking serious sobbing here: shoulders shaking; copious amounts of tears; his voice broken down to a ragged wheeze.

"Sorry," he cried, "I'm so sorry. My wife...she...last night...left me to run off with her boss."

The air seemed to grow thin as if there were too many people in the room.

Except for the poor soul's weeping and the ambient sounds

of drip coffee brewing, we found ourselves suddenly cloaked in a stony silence.

No one knew what to do.

Except for that shift manager.

She took three steps forward, wrapped her arms around the man, and sort of held onto him until he was better.

No one was in a hurry anymore.

It was like watching a well-written drama playing out in front of us with nearly flawless accuracy.

At some point, she led the man over to a table and sat him down, whereupon the guy in line who had shouted at him placed a gentle hand on his shoulder and asked if he could perhaps buy the guy a coffee.

To which the man replied, "Thanks. But they'll probably get the order wrong."

And then he laughed.

We all laughed.

The "soul" of St. Arbuck's is alive and well.

22

The Floor Show

MY wife and I recently spent six weeks in Spain.
Barcelona, to be precise.
Catalunya, to be even more precise.

We were housed in a four bedroom apartment about 50 meters from the Mediterranean in a little resort village called Sitges, 30 km south of Barcelona.

About four days into our stay, we decided to take *el tren* into Barcelona to find a St. Arbuck's and to see Las Ramblas, the street that Victor Hugo (Les Miserables) called *"the most beautiful on earth."*

Beautiful, yes.

The most beautiful on earth?

That's a tough call.

Anyway, that's not what I want to talk about.

I want to talk about the train.

The first thing I learned is that personal hygiene isn't necessarily required for admission.

Enough said.

Anyway, we were well on our way into Barcelona when it began.

I mean who knew there was going to be a floor show on the *Renfe*.

First off, this random woman stands up and starts wailing what I at first thought was a prayer; then perhaps a song; but in the end, I realized she was begging.

Yep!

With a 12 month-old baby strapped to her front side she made her way up and down the aisles of the train holding out a paper cup and giving it a sharp shake when she came by you.

After about ten minutes of her carrying on, she left to go to another section of the train.

Next up, were two Romanian brothers playing accordions.

They were pretty good.

They ran through "Those Were The Days My Friend," a medley from "Fiddler On The Roof," and just when I thought I'd heard it all, they busted out with "Cielito Lindo".

You know, "Aye, yi, yi, yi..." etc.

I mean, come on..."Cielito Lindo" is bad enough when performed as a mariachi song in Old Town San Diego, but Romanian accordion players in Barcelona?

But, like I said, they were good.

In fact, I thought about giving them some money when they passed the hat, or leather pouch in this case.

And then it hit me: is it morally wrong to encourage an accordion player to keep playing?

No, really...is it?

The more I thought about it, the more I wondered if perhaps there wasn't an international law against it or something.

I had visions of me reaching my hand out to drop a coin in the pouch only to feel the cold bite of manacles being slapped around my wrist by a stern-faced Constable saying, "That's it, buddy! Conspiracy to encourage the continuance of accordion music. You'll get five years hard time, minimum! Book him!" The other passengers give me hard stares while I'm being led off the train, my head hung shamefully and muttering, "I'm sorry...I didn't know. Please forgive me."

So just to be safe, I didn't give them a cent!

23

Las Ramblas

WE found a St. Arbuck's on Las Ramblas in downtown Barcelona.

In fact, we managed to find it quite a lot during our stay.

It looks just like the St. Arbuck's by our house in Las Vegas and the one where I hang out when I'm in San Diego.

They have the same cute little hangy-down lights over the coffee bar.

Tables, chairs...the same.

The baristas no less frantic than at home.

I counted fifteen 20-something young people working on laptop computers and totally ignoring everyone around them.

Probably looking on one of those sites designed to help you meet other people with your same interests.

I really wanted to tap this one guy on the shoulder and say, "Excuse me, but do you realize that there are at least ten quite attractive young women your age who are sitting within ten feet of you? Dude...turn off your computer and go talk to them!"

The coffee they serve is a bit stronger, and they don't seem to have even the slightest comprehension as to what "half-n -half" is all about.

Come to think of it, neither do I.

What...it's half cream and half milk?

But isn't milk basically cream that's been watered down?

So you take watered down cream and add real cream to make it cream but not cream?

I'm not getting this.

I bought some actual cream at "Intermarche," the local grocery store about three blocks from our apartment.

It said "38%" on the label.

Someone told me that the number refers to the fat content.

Wow! That's pretty fat.

Maybe there's something to be said for half-n-half after all.

I might have to take an extra Lipitor or something.

24

Tale Of The Ancient Walker

WE sat one particular morning in Barcelona on a low wall overlooking a beach that is a bit out-of-the-way. We were drinking our St. Arbuck's beverages of choice and simply enjoying the experience of being by the Mediterranean. The sky was so clear and the water so reflective of the azure expanse we found ourselves temporarily transfixed by the sight.

The beach was deserted except for a power-walking woman and shirtless elderly man in baggy swim trunks hobbling along the shoreline in an exercise we presumed was an everyday practice for him.

Did I say hobbling?

I should have said tottering, for that is a far better description.

And yet, there he was...enjoying each and every painful and difficult step by a sea he had no doubt spent his entire life observing.

It was touching in its simplicity, profound in its implications.

He reached one end of the stretch of sand, turned and started back in the other direction seemingly oblivious to everything except his exercise.

About a hundred yards away—on the narrow street that bordered the beach—was a film crew setting up on the sidewalk preparing to do something important, at least that was my assumption based on the level of activity we observed.

Possibly, probably, involving a famous actress or an actor or two: you know, movie people...important folks in the eyes of the world.

Yet the old man paid them not the slightest heed, but with his head down, he simply forged ahead in spite of the pain, in spite of the busyness a few yards away.

It made me very aware of the extent to which I defer things simply on the basis of whether they are difficult or not, and I wonder: does the way I approach my life have more to do with ease of passage rather than getting to where I've been called, painful or not?

For this elderly gentleman, I'm guessing that nearly everything in his life is difficult—but not a deterrent.

What I really wanted to do was to intercept the old fellow and inquire about his life and times and by what path he had come to be there on that beach on this beautiful morning.

Of course I didn't.

But I so wanted to if for no other reason than to pass along a heartfelt "thank-you" for providing a moment of inspiration in a world where I find it to be so desperately needed.

25

Barcelona Logic

WE experienced some Barcelona logic recently when we, along with eight other people, attempted to eat lunch at a sidewalk café.

It was close to that St. Arbuck's we visit.

They set up a couple of tables and we squeezed uncomfortably around them.

Noticing one more table nearby, we requested that they set that one up as well.

Witness the following exchange:

Us: "If we had that other table it would be more comfortable for us."

Waiter: "Oh, I cannot give you that table."

Us: "Why not?"

Waiter: "Because it is my last one."

Us: "Right."

Waiter: "What if I gave you the table and someone else came and wanted to sit outside? They couldn't."

Us: "Uhhhhh...uhhhhh..."

Waiter: "So you cannot have the table."

Us: "Uhhhhh...uhhhhh..."

Resolute in his logical stance, he waited to take our order.

It was at that point that my brain exploded, so I can't really tell you how the story ended.

The Storehouse Of Days

I would see him every morning without fail on the patio of
the local St. Arbuck's.
He sat there in the sun, head back, eyes closed simply
breathing...by his side a battered cane that had seen more miles
than many cars I've owned.

A sigh, a rattling cough.

His head seemed to suddenly come unhinged, dropping
first to one side, and then chin to chest only to be jolted back
into position, as if by tiny unseen men with padded poles who
had ringed his chair in anticipation of just such an occurrence.

Sleep finally conquered and he dreamed, snoring softly,
pleasantly.

And I wondered...what filled his dreamscape?

His lips formed a mysterious little half-smile as if in response
to a favorite memory scrolling across his subconscious mind:

Perhaps it was when, as a young man, he'd seen his wife for
the first time.

How the sun had backlit her form as she approached him
over the crest of a low hill, the light dancing off her auburn
hair.

And that smile radiating from her face—the smile in future years he would realize she held in reserve only for him.

His special treasure, his beauty, his lover and constant companion now dead and gone these many years.

Or perhaps he dreamed of holding his first-born in his arms and indulging in a bit of creative imagination as to what life would bring to this red, squalling man-child.

Would he succeed?

Would he find happiness?

Would he find a love like the love his father had found?

Granddaughters clinging to his legs as he "giant-walked" them across the sand and into the surf, their crystalline laughter still ringing in his ears.

Long, lazy afternoon siestas spent with lifelong friends at their special place on the promenade where they could talk of younger days as the sea breeze ruffled the hair on their snowy heads, at once cursing and envying the young folk who frolicked in the same sand and surf where they once played.

His eyes snapped open suddenly catching me in my voyeuristic imaginings.

A long gaze, a nod of his head, a raspy, "Bon dia," and then sleep reclaimed him.

And I wondered, "If I return, old father, will you still be here in your place in the sun? Or will you have followed your beloved; your old friends into the inevitable embrace of eternity?"

I can't tell you why this particular scene filled me with such melancholy, but it did.

It most certainly did.

And I'll never forget that ancient, craggy face nor the way he looked at me with the weight of so many years behind his appraisal as if to say, "Live well, young man...live well, for you too will one day come to where the storehouse of your days holds less than the sum of your memories."

And so I shall.

27

Conversations With Eddie-Part 3

REENTRY into normal life would not be complete without a trip to my very own friendly neighborhood St. Arbuck's, and St. Arbuck's loses something in the experience without Eddie (my disgustingly good-looking, African-American best friend) being there with me.

So I sat there, luxuriating in the sounds, smells and textures feeling somewhat overwhelmed at the "otherness" of it all as compared to what I'd experienced for the past six weeks in Spain.

"So what you gonna' do now that you're back and you don't have the Barcelona thing out there in front of you?" he said absently as a couple of guys from the gym next door passed by leaving an olfactory nightmare in their wake.

Indeed, what am I going to do?

He had posed a question that has, I am ashamed to admit, kept me awake more than a few nights of late.

"Well, first on my list is to finish this coffee," I said partly in jest.

He smiled one of his crooked "you know I can hurt you if I want to" smiles.

"Right...and then what?"

I knew he would not be put off by mere jesting so I said, "If I knew the answer don't you think I'd tell you?"

"Maybe."

"What do you mean, maybe?"

His large soy latte was halted halfway to his lips and he said, "You are sometimes quite forthcoming with information and at other times, well, you ain't."

My lips parted of their own accord in anticipation of the dismissive reply that had already formed in my caffeine saturated brain.

But I didn't say it because I knew he was right.

"Do you always have to be right?"

"Can't help it if I'm insightful," he said and then took a long drink of his foul brew.

"All right, since you've probably got this all figured out anyway I will tell you that there are a number of things we are considering for the future. Among them, staying right where we are and continuing to write and just enjoy life."

"And what else?"

I sighed because I really didn't want to go into it.

But I knew he wouldn't leave me alone until I did.

"That thing in San Diego is still a possibility as is the possibility of investigating other opportunities in Europe like the one we just completed."

He sat there with his lips pressed together slowly nodding his head.

"So what do you want to do?"

"What do I want to do?"

"Yeah, you know if money was no object and you could do anything you wanted...what would it be?"

Man! I hate questions like that.

"When I resigned back in June I thought I had that all figured out."

"I know you did," he said in measured tones. "But it's not what you thought, is it?"

"No. I mean, don't get me wrong, I love the freedom of getting up every day and doing whatever suits me."

"But..."

"But I really need to be around people; to feel a sense of being influential in their lives; to do things that make you feel like you matter."

He wrinkled his brow and said, "Oh, don't worry none about that, RG, you matter to plenty of people."

"And then there's the music."

"You miss it."

I paused to watch two teenaged girls pass by with iPods in their ears, thumbs flying over the faceplates of their cellular phones dashing off text messages while at the same time talking in rapid fire teenspeak to each other.

"Yeah, and playing with the band in Barcelona only reinforced how much."

He sighed and said, "I repeat...what are you gonna' do?"

"All along we've believed that there is a new season being blown into our lives, and at this point it's just a matter of discovering what that is." I shook my head and said, "I've never been this paralyzed by indecision before."

"You know how you're always saying that sometimes before you can experience the miraculous you will often have to do something that is completely ridiculous?"

Nothing worse than having a good line quoted back to you.

"All right, I'll bite. What's your point?"

"You've already done the ridiculous."

"You mean resigning my position?"

"Uh-huh," he said, drawing the syllables out dramatically. "Now it's time to experience the miraculous."

He was right, and I knew he was right.

28

The Muse

I'VE observed him from my corner.

He's there several times a week.

Twenty-something.

Shaved head.

Big, black glasses with lots of plastic.

No. 2 pencil in hand.

Unlined journal opened before him.

Large latte with three add-shots on the table.

He does a lot of staring.

I've got him figured for a songwriter.

And though I've never spoken to him, I know what he's doing.

Waiting for the Muse.

It's a common pastime for those of us cursed—or blessed, depending on one's perspective—with a creative vein.

Today he's actually written something down on the white, virginal pages of his journal.

It's an oddity.

Believe me.

Mostly, he never quite gets around to putting down on paper what he's hearing in his head.

Pity.

"Songwriter?" I finally ask on my way to use the public convenience.

"What? Oh, yeah. I suppose," he said somewhat grimly.

"Mind if I sit for a minute?"

"No," he said. "Please."

I sat.

"So, how long have you been writing?"

He thought for a moment.

"Uh, let's see...maybe two years."

"And are you in a band?" I queried.

This brought a laugh.

"And that was funny because..." I prompted.

"Well, it's a long story, but the bottom line is that my band was interested in getting and staying drunk, while I, on the other hand, was interested in actually creating music."

I nodded.

"A sad but common story."

"So I've heard. And now, I've got no one. So I come here day after day and pretend like I'm still doing something creative," he said bitterly.

I leaned my elbows on the tabletop.

"Nah, man. There's no pretense here. You are creative." I tapped his journal. "I've watched you."

"What...this?" he said as he held up the journal and then dropped it onto the table. "This is nothing but the mad ravings of a broken-hearted fool."

I knew what he was talking about.

For among the young and passionate, there is nothing quite so filled with potential heartbreak—aside from romance—as there is in the formation and inevitable dissolution of a band.

Why?

The sacrifices people are willing to make for the purpose of perpetuating a band often defy logic.

It's mainly about that "band of brothers" thing.

You know, "We started this thing together and we'll stay together no matter what the cost."

I understand this sentiment and even appreciate it on some level.

When I worked for a record label, we rarely signed the entire band to a recording contract.

Why?

Because bands tend to break up!

So, here he sits.

Day after day.

Trying to recapture something of the magic he felt working with his band mates.

"You ever thought of going solo?" I said.

A small smile and then, "Oddly enough, I AM solo whether I want to be or not."

"Oh, sooner or later you'll discover that it actually isn't that bad."

"Another thing I keep telling myself."

We both laughed and I stood and started to walk away only to be stopped by, "Hey! What's your name?"

"RG," said I.

"Next time you're in, RG, can I buy you a coffee."

"Only if you promise to show me some of your songs."

He nodded in satisfaction.

"You got yourself a deal."

29

Joie De Vivre

AS with some things that are factual and require no discussion to be so affirmed, it is a fact that sunsets are meant to be experienced on the westernmost shores of the 48 contiguous states.

There is just something about being on the beach with your sweetheart, sitting, standing, lying down—the posture is basically irrelevant—while the sun makes its slow and deliberate descent into the bosom of the Pacific.

You can watch it every day, as some have been known to do, and never lose the wonder.

And every day at sunset along the Southern California coast in San Diego County, clustered in choice settings, groups of people stand mesmerized by the celestial display, many having planned their whole schedule around being able to be there for that special moment.

I thought about all of this as I strolled along the beach and watched the last sliver of gold slip below the horizon.

The dusky-hued twilight shoreline, filled with others sharing a similar compulsion for a sunset stroll, took on a magical quality.

I'm not sure why, but I always find myself exchanging greetings with these sunset walkers as if they were old friends, even though most are total strangers.

I reached Tamarack beach, the end of my route and turned my steps away from the shoreline, walking through the deep sand to the stairs that led past the lifeguard tower to the paved walkway behind the sea wall.

Up another flight of stairs were public facilities and an outside shower nozzle used mainly by surfers to rinse sand and salt water off of wetsuits, boards and bodies.

I headed north along the brightly lit sidewalk which runs along the boulevard marveling as I often do at the large number of fellow walkers, joggers, bikers and skaters who frequent this route; people from all walks of life and every generation.

There was the elderly couple from the retirement community in the village, shuffling slowly along but holding hands as if they were still in their twenties, the light of love burning brightly in their eyes; young professional people who jogged or skated by singly and in pairs, some married with children and others obviously at the beginning of new relationships; middle-aged couples enjoying the fruit of their investments talking excitedly about future adventures.

Then there were the surfers, with the top half of their wetsuits pulled down around their waists and carrying themselves with a pleasant weariness, their faces sun and wind burned and bearing smiles of affable camaraderie.

With surfboards held loosely under their arms they chatted animatedly about waves they had "shredded" and the ones that got away as their feet, still dripping salt water, left a trail of footprints—a trail that had been followed by many who had gone before.

Groups of teenage boys orbited hopefully and compulsively around groups of teenage girls awkwardly seeking to win their attention.

This scene always brings a smile to my face, as it doesn't seem so very long ago that I had been one of those poor hormonally tortured wretches.

They would learn soon enough that girls are incomprehensible creatures, jointly and severally dedicated to insuring that each and every pubescent male endures the compulsory amount of adolescent angst.

I passed what my wife and I call our "funny little fish place" and celebrated for the thousandth time in the past month the simple joy of being alive, realizing that what I really needed right then was a cuppa' Joe.

And wouldn't you know it...St. Arbuck's was right across the street.

It just gets better and better.

30

Sunrise

THE beach is deserted.

The air is salt-scented and heavy with mist.

The sky is overcast with a promise of clearing by ten AM.

The weathermen call it "June gloom."

I call it bliss.

I run.

I think.

I watch.

I cherish the moment.

My legs, though leaden, churn through the deep sand carrying me relentlessly toward my goal: Saint Arbucks, the place of my morning oblation where I will celebrate the hoisting of the ritual medium coffee with room for cream.

Almost there.

Another hundred yards.

Suddenly, a sound.

Behind me.

Heavy breathing.

Coming up fast.

Passing me.

It's Eddie!

A sideways glance.

Down goes the gauntlet.

I am spent, yet some unknown source of energy propels me forward.

I draw even with the mad sprinter.

His dreads swing rhythmically.

Dark skin glistening with moisture.

Perfect, white teeth bared in a grimace known to runners far and wide.

The stakes are high.

Loser pays.

Neck and neck we fly toward the patio.

The regulars stand, caught in rapt attention as we strain for the edge of the concrete.

Done.

I win today.

"And the crowd went wild."

Arms about one another's shoulders we stagger to the counter, neither of us possessing sufficient wind to order.

"Aren't you guys too old for this?" asks the cute but discourteous barista.

"He (gasp) he (gasp) he (gasp) is," says Eddie. "I...I...I'm just fine."

"Yeah, you look it," says she, sliding our brews across the counter. "Want me to carry these to the table for you?"

Snatching up our coffees we head for our usual table.

"Tomorrow," he says bravely. "I'll get you tomorrow."

With a wink and a smile I drink my brew, satisfied in the fact that I remain champion...if only for today.

31

About Birds and Stuff-Part 2

O N a late summer's morning, I sat with my beloved on the patio of our favorite St. Arbuck's doing what we normally do on normal days, to whit, reading the paper, doing sudoku, sipping our beverages of choice and sort of easing into the morning.

Without warning the patio was invaded by a group of fluttering ruffians, also known as pigeons, the most foul of all fowl in my humble opinion.

Little better than flying rats, the brash creatures set about casing the joint.

You've seen it before.

They approach your table as if to say, "Hand over the pastries and no one will get hurt."

I always imagine this being spoken in a deep, Brooklynese brogue.

Just as I was preparing to make a move to scatter the gang of scavenging cutthroats, I noticed something unusual in their midst...two young sparrows.

I said to my wife, "Look at that."

She looked, nodded sadly and said, "They've fallen in with a rough crowd. Their mothers must be heartbroken."

I thought about that image for a moment: a weeping sparrow mother perched high in a tree, her eyes scanning the horizion and singing mournfully, *"Oh where is my wandering boy tonight; down at the corner saloon."*

I locked eyes—well, in his case, eye—with the scamp who appeared to be the leader.

It was a staredown.

A standoff.

And I wasn't about to lose, not to a lowlife like this dirty bird.

One of the sparrows hopped over and stood next to him, sort of twittering as if to say, "What're we doin' now, Spike? Are we gonna' get the food, huh, Spike?"

"Spike," of course, didn't want to answer for to do so would've meant breaking off our staring contest, so he kind of brushed the kid aside with his wing while maintaining eye contact with me.

The kid went sprawling and hopped up quickly, shaking his head in confusion.

Beads of sweat appeared on Spike's brow...okay, I'm making this part up, but just go with it.

He began to tremble under the exertion, finally staggering backwards, victim to my superior willpower.

Spike, the vanquished, hopped sadly away without so much as a backward glance.

The two youngsters looked at Spike, and then at me; Spike; me; Spike; me, and finally, in a remarkable display of good sense, hopped over to my table where they sat staring up at me with loving fealty.

My beloved said, "It looks as if you made a couple of new fans."

"Lucky me."

I tossed them each a generous portion of pastry for which they thanked me by snatching up in their beaks and flying away never to be seen again.

"Well," she said, "at least their mothers will thank you."

Like I said, lucky me.

32

Conversations With
Eddie-Part 4

THE four of us sat around a fire pit on the patio of a funky, beachside St. Arbuck's sipping our brew of choice as a somewhat less than adequate acoustic trio, consisting of two guitars and an upright bass, provided low level background music.

After my wife and I made firm plans to go to San Diego for the weekend, my disgustingly good-looking African-American best friend Eddie, and his equally lovely wife Sylvie, decided to meet us there.

"So, maybe we confiscate those instruments before the boys hurt themselves," Eddie intoned seriously as the trio launched into a bellowing rendition of Tom Petty's, "I Won't Back Down."

Sylvie slapped him on the arm.

"Do you always have to be so cynical?"

He glanced knowingly in my direction and said, "It's not cynicism. It's self-preservation!"

He was right.

The trio was nearly unbearable.

I said, "I suppose we could requisition their stuff and regale the assemblage with our own adroit and dexterous interpretation."

Sylvie screwed up her face and said, "What?"

Eddie provided, "He said he and I should play the song."

"Then why didn't he just say that?"

"Sounded better the way he said it."

Cheri laughed.

"You get used to it after awhile."

It was a beautiful evening.

The winds had died down giving way to clear skies and temperatures in the low seventies.

We had arrived in time to get checked into our rooms and go for a quick walk on the beach at sunset.

The sunset was a good one.

Of course, now that I think of it, I've never seen one I'd judge as being "bad."

Eddie was staring increduously at the group.

"Maybe if I tip them handsomely, they'd go home for the evening."

"No," said I, "It'd just encourage them to play louder and longer."

Sylvie said, "Come on, you two, they're not that bad."

Eddie and I exchanged glances.

"Right," we said in unison, drawing it out dramatically.

Thankfully they finished the set and announced a twenty-minute break.

The bass player walked in our direction, a look of recognition on his face.

"R.G.?" he said as he neared our table.

I looked at him with no scrap of recognition.

"Yes?"

"It's Bill. You remember—from Bridge Over Darkness?" He

smiled widely revealing an orthodontist's retirement residing inside his mouth.

"Okay. Refresh my memory."

Uninvited, he pulled up a chair.

"Yeah, we recorded with you a few years back."

All at once the memory returned.

"So, I take it the band didn't make it?"

He shook his head sadly.

"Nah, man. It just wasn't the right mix of personalities. Different directions musically—you know the drill."

Indeed I did.

As I've said before, bands tend to break up.

"Happens a lot. So, what's this?" I asked, gesturing to the other members of the trio.

He followed my gaze.

"Oh, this. It's nothing, really. Just something to do to keep my chops up. And how about you? Still producing?"

"Yeah." I didn't really want to get into a recitation of all that was happening in my life, so I settled on, "Mainly doing my own thing."

He smiled genuinely.

"Good. That's real good. You were the best producer we ever worked with."

For some reason the compliment felt good.

"Thanks, Bill."

I took a minute and introduced Cheri and the others.

Handshakes were exchanged all around.

"Well, listen, I've got to get back. It was nice to meet you folks, and real nice to see you again."

Eddie said, "Break a leg, but don't break a string."

He laughed good-naturedly as he returned to his band mates, gesturing in our direction as if we were celebrities or something.

Eddie noticed that my mood had suddenly turned pensive.

"Okay. What's wrong?"

I just shook my head sadly.

"I don't know. I guess I just had a vision of this guy that was profoundly unsettling."

Sylvie said, "How so?"

"Well, it's hard to explain. Bill is, what, forty, forty-five?"

"'Bout that," Eddie said as Cheri and Sylvie nodded their agreement.

I pondered my next thought.

"He was once young and filled with dreams and a fierce ambition. In fact, at the time I produced their demo the dreams were still very much alive."

Cheri knows me well enough to understand where I was going.

"And now he's empty?"

I leaned forward, elbows on my knees, warming my hands in front of the fire pit.

"Yeah, but it's a different kind of empty. There's an empty that comes from being poured out," I glanced at Eddie, "like at the end of a really good show where you've given it all you had."

Sylvie said hurriedly, "Let me take a crack at this. The other kind of empty is the one where life has just sucked it all out of you to the point that there's nothing left." She paused for a moment and then said, "How'd I do?"

"You just described Bill," I said. "This is the reason I got out of the music business. Stuff like this just tears me up."

"Not your fault, my man," Eddie said encouragingly.

"Maybe not, but it always feels like it is."

The trio started their next set.

Sylvie said, "You guys ready to go?"

Eddie and I looked at each other.

Eddie said, "How about we stay and enjoy the music for a bit."

33

Faded Around
The Edges

THE clapboard sign was faded around the edges.
Perched atop an equally distressed structure I could see it clearly from my carefully chosen spot on the patio of a beachside St. Arbuck's.

Advertised thereupon was something about paint, but I was too distracted to pay much heed to the message.

It was that "faded around the edges" thing.

You see, I've been feeling much the same of late and it bothers me.

It bothers me quite a lot, if you want to know the truth.

My Grandfather was past seventy when I was born, so in all my memories he is an old man.

But it wasn't always so.

My uncle, now an octogenarian himself, told me recently that as a young man Grandpa had been a pitcher, and a good one at that—good enough to play with some of the best baseball players of his day.

I found myself utterly stunned by the revelation for

121

nowhere in my conscious mind did there exist a memory to accommodate my Grandfather as anything other than a dirt poor sharecropper—a simple mountain man from the Ozarks.

One who had moved his family West during the "dust bowl" and Depression years of the 1930's in hopes of starting over in the golden, balmy climes of coastal California.

In so doing, baseball and any chance for a different life than that experienced by the four generations of men who had gone before him, had been left behind.

By the time I met my grandfather the years had taken their toll and only faint lines remained of the bold strokes which had once etched the life of a strong and passionate man.

So there I sat, transfixed by that derelict of a sign wishing I could have known the man in his prime.

Wishing I could have watched him throw a curve ball.

Wishing I could have done anything with him that would have demonstrated his former strength.

Faded around the edges.

Can I just be honest for a moment?

You want to know what I really wish?

I wish that those who meet me *now* for the first time could have known me *when,* instead of this guy whose edges are, if not faded, very definitely frayed.

The sad truth is I mourn the loss of that feisty, passionate youth that got me into so much trouble and yet carried me so far.

I thought about all of this, took a sip of my medium coffee with room for cream and stared at the sign some more.

As is often the case, my ruminations were interrupted by a one word thought.

"Multiplied."

I struggled for comprehension.

The thought continued with, "The years that remain can

be multiplied sufficiently to surpass the years that have already been spent. It's your choice."

In the silence that followed, I felt the warm and tender fingers of understanding as they massaged this truth into my conscious mind.

And it was good.

It was so good.

I finished my coffee, walked across the street and got a little closer to the sign.

I suddenly realized it wasn't nearly as faded as I had at first perceived.

It was more, well, weathered.

The realization made me smile, for fading happens when something has been left out in the sun too long.

But being weathered can only come about as a result of having withstood the storm.

I walked away feeling positively brilliant.

34

Crooked Canyons

I grew up on the Monterey Bay—about 75 miles south of San Francisco—in a small central California beach community where the mountains kissed the sea...and we were right in the middle of the smack!

I know it's corny, but I couldn't help myself.

It was a place where each morning was gently caressed by wispy tendrils of fog that wound their way over and through the redwood-forested foothills.

A place where the sun rarely made its appearance before noon and then, peeking through the fog, brushed the earth only briefly before retreating behind the verdant hills; a place where sand and surf was only minutes away...that is if one possessed a bicycle as formidable as "The Green Hornet," my slim-tired, racing-handle-barred, hand-braked, ten-speeded wonder.

Most often leisure time would find me at the helm of my faithful green steed.

Together we flew over the emerald slopes on crooked two-lane roadways, carefree and energetic in the perpetual pursuit of boyish fantasy.

It was a good life.

I've never gotten over smelling the salt air every morning nor have I lost the wonder of staring far past the blue horizon for hours at a time, envisioning myself in some magical adventure.

I lived in a single-parent home and we were quite poor, my mom and I, so pleasures had to be cheap or you had none at all, and the beach was an endless source of pleasure.

"Surf City" was what they called my town and as a teenager I was obsessed with surfing.

Oh, I was never any good.

But, I definitely looked the part—hair, longish and bleached blonde by the sun; skin bronzed and salt-flecked; huarache sandals and a Volkswagen Bug with a long board jutting comically from the tiny window.

Each and every sentence prefaced by, "Dude..." (Spoken, of course, with a slight vocal quiver).

And I said, "Stoked" a lot.

I don't know why.

I spent my collegiate years at a small parochial university about a thirty minute drive up into the mountains.

It was as if the founders had come upon a singularly beautiful spot in the middle of a thick redwood forest and said, "Okay, let's build it here."

They cleared away just enough of the forest to accommodate the structures and today I am quite sure that the property is worth a phenomenal amount of money.

I was a horrible student, mainly because I was too busy working on my "career."

Being in four bands was distraction enough, but I also spent a lot of time recording up in San Francisco.

But it was there at that little university that I met my wife.

I will never forget the first time I saw her walking across the quad.

The earth paused in its orbit; everything within my field of vision blurred except for her image; and when she turned toward me and smiled...angelic hosts spilled over heaven's edge and filled the atmosphere with joyous song.

Well, not really, but you get the idea.

I mean, I am a writer after all.

If you want to know the truth, she still has that same effect on me today.

We got married in the middle of our senior year—something I wouldn't recommend to anyone, by the way—and began our great adventure.

And what an adventure it's been.

"Your coffee's getting cold," said my wife softly snapping me out of my momentary musing.

"What? Oh..." I said as I reconnected to my surroundings—a quite busy St. Arbuck's on a late Friday morning.

She smiled knowingly and said, "Traveling again?"

She knows me well.

"Uh, yeah. Just visiting some old friends."

She went back to her sudoku and I took a long, satisfying drink of my medium coffee with room for cream.

Of late, my mind has been traversing those crooked canyons of memory, pulling up things long since set aside—not on the basis of a particular need, but simply because there are things I never want to forget.

Like that day on the quad.

35

Conversations With Eddie-Part 5

S O, what's the best day you've ever had?

I sat with my disgustingly good-looking African-American best friend Eddie looking out over the broad expanse of sand that stretched between the blue Pacific and our position on the patio of our favorite beachside St. Arbuck's.

"You mean besides today," I said, rolling the greatly diminished contents of my iced tea lemonade and listening to the light tinkling of the ice cubes mingled with the sound of the surf.

It's a sound I love.

Eddie said, "Okay, besides today."

I had to think hard to come up with something.

And for the record, "hard" anything was not on my agenda on this day or any day in the near future.

"Well, there was that one time when we were—"

"No, not we," he said somewhat impatiently. "You. Just you by yourself. The best day."

That made it even more difficult.

"Are you trying to ruin my afternoon?"

"Just answer the question," he said petulantly.

"I think it was in Israel. In Netanya. I spent a Sunday all by myself walking on the beach, strolling through shops, soaking up the sun and just being overwhelmed by the antiquity of the land upon which I trod."

He looked at me in that funny way of his: slightly crooked smile, eyes dancing with mischief.

"Sometimes I forget you're a writer."

"And that is apropos to what?" I queried.

"The way you express yourself. Most folk prob'ly think it a mite strange."

"How so?"

"You tend to go around the barn a lot," he said laughing softly.

I thought about it.

Maybe he was right.

Maybe I do take longer to get places than others.

"And this is a problem for you?"

"No. It's not a problem for me. Just think it's kinda' cute is all."

"Am I being made fun of?" I asked, purposely dangling an innocent preposition.

He said, "When Eddie be makin' fun of someone, they know they bein' made fun of."

"Is there a point to this conversation?"

I really wanted to know as my brain was beginning to protest.

"Just interested in your life. It's why I asked the question."

By now the question was long gone from my memory and I said as much.

"You know," he prompted. "The best day."

"Oh, right. Well, it would have to be that one in Netanya."

Growing suddenly serious he dropped his usual urban

brogue and said, "I know you're struggling right now, and if you need to lean a little, I'll be there for you."

I found the expressed sentiment so startling that it took me a moment to frame a suitable response.

After a few seconds I said, "Thanks, Eddie. I appreciate it...I really do."

He smiled wickedly.

"Enough to buy dinner?"

36

The Heartbreaker

EYES full of wonder, she stood in front of the cooler staring at the vast array of drink selections.

The managed chaos of an unusually busy Friday morning at St. Arbuck's swirled around her unnoticed.

Five or six years old.

Curly black hair.

Porcelain skin set off by a little button mouth with ruby red lips.

Well on her way to being a heartbreaker.

She cast her eyes briefly in my direction, grinned and turned away as if embarrassed by the contact.

"Daphne," came a mother's impatient plea from the register. "Hurry up and pick something."

"I can't!" she wailed. "There's too many."

"There are a lot of people waiting to order. Now come on, we don't have all day."

"Mom," said Daphne, stretching out the single syllable into, "Maw-awhm!"

"You heard me, little missy...let's go."

Daphne sighed and opened the door to the cooler.

With her left index finger firmly affixed in the corner of her mouth, she reached for a bottle, drew her hand back; reached for something else, drew her hand back; reached yet again only to have the same result.

"I can't," she said turning around to stare hopelessly at her mom, who, by now, had abandoned her place in line and was walking purposefully over to deal with her indecisive daughter.

"Why do you do this to me?" she said disgustedly.

"I can't help it if they put so much stuff in there," Daphne said in her defense.

The mom gave me a long-suffering look, and with a shake of her head squatted down so as to be on Daphne's level.

"Look, you know you're going to get the same thing you always get. So why don't you just get it and we can be on our way?"

Daphne looked at her mom, and then at the drinks inside of the cooler.

"But what if I want something else this time?"

"Fine," said mom. "Whatever you want. Just pick something."

"Okay," Daphne said reluctantly.

Mother and daughter turned their collective attention to the cooler and after several minutes of thorough investigation Daphne finally made her selection.

"I told you!" said mom, who stood to her feet and said to me, "Same thing she always gets. What a surprise."

Daphne turned toward me and held up her drink as if for my approval.

I gave her a thumbs-up and a smile.

When they turned back to reenter the line, they found that it stretched literally out the door, which caused mom no small amount of consternation.

"Great!" she said. "Look at the line. Now we're going to be late for sure."

Undaunted, Daphne took her drink and marched boldly toward the front of the line where she stood next to a business man who was, uh, busy talking on his iPhone.

Yanking on his pants leg she said, "Hey."

Following a hasty, "Just a minute," spoken into his phone he looked down and said somewhat impatiently, "Yes?"

"Can I have cuts?" Daphne said sweetly.

At first he looked at her and then at her mom with an, "Are you kidding?" expression, which slowly melted into one that said, "You can have anything you want, sweetheart," after he experienced the full force of her smile.

He motioned with his hand that Daphne should go in front of him while saying to the barista, "Looks like you've got a paying customer here."

Mumbling a hasty apology Daphne's mom paid for her drink, apologized to the man again who assured her that it was absolutely no problem.

As for Daphne, she turned, smiled up at the man and said, "Thanks, mister." Then she leaned around a merchandise table, smiled and waved good-bye to me, returning my "thumbs-up," and led her mother out of the store having logged yet another conquest.

Did I say a "future" heartbreaker?

37

Alone Together

THEY sat in stony silence at a corner window of St. Arbuck's, the emptiness in their eyes seemingly reflective of the emptiness in their lives.

Alone together.

Coffee cups, cell phones and purse clustered in the center of the table like a hastily constructed barricade behind which each sought some form of refuge.

The tension between these two seemed to roll off in waves; at least that's the way it felt from where I sat some ten feet away.

If one were to judge by appearance alone, the man looked to be a thirty-something professional with an expensive haircut, stylish clothing and designer eyeglasses.

He fidgeted incessantly, one leg crossed over another, foot swinging as if possessed of a life of its own, fingers drumming out a crazy rhythm on the tabletop.

The woman, his sartorial equal, was a dusky-haired, natural beauty—a rarity in a city where even high school students are cosmetically enhanced.

Her pale blue eyes flicked toward me and quickly away, but

in that instant, I saw a depth of sadness that struck me like a physical blow.

She leaned back in her chair, stared at the ceiling and then let her head come forward heavily while breathing out a long, tortured sigh.

Turning his gaze away from the window, he drew a deep breath as if to speak, seemed to think better of it and then picked up his cell phone.

After fussing with a few buttons, he tossed it back onto the table and redirected his gaze toward the patio.

I started to wonder where it all had gone wrong and, naturally, who was to blame.

It reminded me of the words to Carole King's fabulous, *Now And Forever*:

I miss the tears
I miss the laughter
I miss the day we met and all that followed after
Sometimes I wish I could always be with you
The way we used to do

And suddenly, I was wiping away a tear hoping that no one saw my inopportune display of emotion, and then just as suddenly, I found that I didn't care.

Because it hurt me.

It hurt me deeply to see these two young strangers, so blessed with good looks and obvious financial success...yet so devoid of true happiness.

Then, out of the corner of my eye, I saw a cautious movement from the man's side of the table.

He reached his hand slowly, tentatively toward her hand where it rested lifelessly on the tabletop.

When she realized what he was doing, it seemed that she was going to jerk her hand away, but then she seemed to reconsider.

And when his hand covered hers, while no words were spoken something passed between them.

Something which required no words.

One heart reaching out to another.

They gazed into each other's eyes for a long moment, and then both hands joined and they leaned toward each other, their lips meeting directly over the aforementioned barricade.

And then they kissed.

Not so much a kiss of passion, as it was of, well, more like, "I've just missed you so much."

Yeah.

Like that.

They both glanced my way and, not knowing what else to do I gave them a sincere smile.

Nodding a silent, "Thank-you," and smiling as if to say, "We're going to be okay," they gathered up their things and went on their way.

And I thought to myself, *"Is this a happy ending I've just seen?"*

One can hope.

38

Conversations With
Eddie-Part 6

EDDIE and I sat in our usual spot.

It's right over there in the corner by the condiment bar.

St. Arbuck's was characteristically busy and the line to purchase coffee stretched literally out the door causing many regulars to turn around and stomp angrily back to their car without even coming in.

We sat and watched the flow of busy people coming and going for a bit before he yawned and said, "Haven't been sleeping well at all."

"Really?" said I. "Why not?"

He cocked one eyebrow at me, kind of like that wrestler guy-turned-action-adventure-hero, The Rock.

"That's a silly question."

"And why would you say that?"

"Because if I knew why I wasn't sleeping, don't you think I'd fix the problem?"

I suggested, "Maybe it's your sheets."

"Nothin' wrong with my sheets," he said, adding proudly, "for your information they're five-hundred thread count."

I chuckled.

"What's so funny?" he said defensively.

"Five-hundred thread count? You think that's good?"

"Course it's good. Why, you got something better?"

Actually, I did.

"Yeah, I mean I don't want to boast, but we don't sleep on anything less than eight-hundred thread count Egyptian cotton."

He was obviously unprepared for such extravagance.

"Come on now, you're not serious."

"I am absolutely serious. In fact, we just got a great deal on a thousand thread count."

"A thousand?"

I nodded an affirmation while taking a long, slow sip of my medium coffee with room for cream.

He seemed positively crestfallen.

"And here I been braggin' about my little five-hundreds."

I started to reply when suddenly a look of near panic came over his face.

He looked all around our immediate area as if attempting to ascertain if anyone had overheard our conversation.

"Dude," he said seriously. "Here we are two grown men, sitting out in public talking about the thread count in our bed linens!"

I saw nothing wrong with it and said as much.

He leaned across the table and said in a pronounced stage-whisper, "Nothing wrong? People overhear us and they think we a couple of metrosexuals!"

"But, we're not, right? I mean, right?" I said as the first trickle of sweat crawled its way across my forehead.

"People examine the facts in evidence, Jack, it'd be hard to muster a defense."

He was right.

"Look, we are not metrosexuals...but just the same, no more discussions involving bed linen."

"Heard that!" he said as he stood to go.

"Metrosexuals...that's the dumbest thing I ever heard," I muttered while straightening my Dolce & Gabbana glasses and checking my image in my wrist mirror.

39

Ma Fille Speciale

ON a beautiful, sun-kissed San Diego Saturday, I sat outside my favorite St. Arbuck's with the plaintive cries of the gulls filling my ears and the salt air stinging my nose ever so slightly.

It was a great day for doing not much of anything, an enterprise at which I excel.

I saw her across the broad patio long before she saw me.

An arrestingly attractive young lady sitting alone.

She held an acoustic guitar in her hands, glancing at the method book lying open on the table in front of her and then at the painfully held chord position on the neck.

Then she played...badly.

To anyone who didn't know her—especially men—she looked like just another beauty among the multitudes that populate San Diego county.

Perhaps a model, or someone they'd seen decorating the face of a billboard.

But I had a different perspective.

You see, I'd known her since she was eight.

Next month she turns twenty.

Makes me feel even older than I am.

She had been in a community children's chorus that I directed at the time and had also studied piano and voice under my tutelage.

More than once I remembered thinking that she was special; that she had that "it" factor you hear so much about these days; that with the proper nurture and direction she could really go far.

Maybe even have a shot at a recording career.

So I took my medium coffee and sat at a table not far from where she waged war with the instrument.

For a few moments, she was lost in deep concentration.

Then, her head came up.

She looked right at me.

At first, there was no recognition in her eyes.

Then there was.

"Oh!" she gasped. "Oh, my gosh!"

She dropped her guitar and ran across the space that separated us almost leaping into my waiting hug.

She held on to me as if her life depended on it.

And then, she cried.

I didn't know why.

"I can't believe you're here," she said, stepping back and holding me at arm's length.

"Well, I'm here most every day," I said as I followed her over to her table.

"No, I mean I can't believe you're here today."

"Because..." I prompted.

She sat, bowing her head and crying some more.

"Because I don't know what to do."

Her exquisitely sculpted face seemed to collapse in on itself.

Her shoulders sagged; tresses spilling out from underneath

the stylish baseball cap, falling in a tangle around her shoulders.

"Hey," I said softly. "Tell me what's happening."

I hadn't seen her for almost two years.

She closed her eyes.

"I don't think I can."

I sat back.

"Why don't you try?"

She inhaled, and then blew out a long breath of air.

"I'm kind of involved in something; something not real good."

I already didn't like where this was going, but I remained quiet.

"See, I got this job. It's a, well, you know, not exactly something I'm proud of. But the money is so great and..."

"What are you doing?" I asked as gently as possible.

Eyes closed and shoulders shaking with sobs she said, "I'm a dancer!"

At first, I didn't get it, but suddenly her pronouncement became crystal clear.

A dancer.

One of *those* dancers.

I had been prepared for a lot of things, but not that.

I could feel the flood building behind my own eyes, but I managed to hold it in check as visions of a sweet little girl filled my mind.

"Well," I said, simply because nothing else came to mind. "That's, uh—"

"Do you hate me?" she said in a rush, eyes pleading.

I wondered what her late father would have said to her right at that instant.

I made a decision.

"Of course I don't hate you. I just hope that you're not being forced into this."

Her eyes looked far away for a moment and then back.

"When I was a little girl, you used to tell me all the time that I was your special girl. Remember that?"

I did.

And she had been.

No father; mother addicted to serial monogamy.

And I had been determined that there would be at least one man in her life who would care for her because of who she was and not for what they could get from her.

"Yes, I remember."

"Well, do you still think I'm special?"

I held her gaze until unbidden the tears came, arcing downward across my sun-roughened skin.

"Special," I said, "is because of who you are...not because of what you do or do not do."

A sob escaped her throat and she reached out, grasping my hands as if in a death grip.

Then, we both cried.

A lot.

And then we were through crying.

"Listen," I said. "What do you need from me right now?"

She thought about it and then said, "I have to find a way out of this lifestyle. It's...killing me." She paused, eyes blinking rapidly. "The men...they...no one ever looks at my eyes, my face. To them I'm just a piece of meat."

Suddenly her name was called loudly from somewhere behind me.

I turned and spotted a rough looking young man in dark glasses with full-sleeve tattoos covering both arms.

"Would you come on, already? I don't have all day!" he said impatiently.

Quickly gathering up her guitar and method book she shot me a terrified look and said, "Look, I'm sorry. I, uh, I've got to go."

She started to walk away but turned back and said, "It was good seeing you. Really, really good."

And then she was gone.

A seagull swooped down and picked up the broken remnants of her pastry.

It made me wonder if one day someone would be called upon to do the same with her life.

As I watched her walk across the parking lot and climb into an expensive SUV, somewhere in the canyons of my memory I could hear her eight year-old voice singing, *"The sun'll come out tomorrow; bet your bottom dollar that tomorrow there'll be sun..."*

40

Random Encounters

I was reading through a recently completed page on my computer screen when a young man caught my attention. He sat in the corner in one of two overstuffed chairs for which St. Arbuck's has become famous.

He was nervous.

My first clue was the nearly compulsive way he checked first his watch and then his cell phone about every seven seconds.

Back and forth.

Watch.

Cell phone.

Watch.

You get the picture.

If I had to guess his age I'd say he was in his mid to late twenties.

Good looking kid and reasonably well dressed.

I began to play one of my favorite guessing games.

I call it, "Can you guess why he's here?"

This one was going to be easy...Job interview.

Had to be.

On the small table between his chair and its twin was a medium sized booklet.

To break up the monotony of the watch/cell phone thing, he would pick up the booklet, thumb through it and then set it back down on the table.

This was done no less than a dozen times.

I saw him look up expectantly as the door opened to admit a couple of guys in suits.

He made a motion as if he were going to stand, hesitated, and then stood only to quickly sit back down.

By this time the two suits were in line awaiting a chance to order.

He looked at the two, then at the booklet; fiddled with his cell phone as if a call were coming in, or perhaps he was preparing to dial out; checked his watch; looked at the suits...

He glanced my way and gave me a little half-smile and blew out a big breath of air.

I returned the smile with a nod of my head as if to say, "Go for it."

He stood and took up a position where the suits would literally have to run him over to get out of the place.

They almost did.

Walked right by him without even so much as a glance.

He watched them go, his mouth opening and closing like a big-mouthed bass that has just landed on the alien surface of a boat deck and is slowly starving for oxygen.

He turned around, saw me and muttered through an embarrassed grin, "Guess they weren't the right guys."

It was then that I saw the wedding ring.

He sat down and placed a call.

I overheard him say, "Hi baby. No, not yet. Couple of guys just came in but it wasn't them. They're 30 minutes late already, how long should I wait?"

He paused as if listening to the reply.

"Okay. But if this doesn't work out, I don't know what else to do."

After a moment or two he said tenderly, "Listen, I'm just going to come home. Something will come up. We'll be all right."

Snapping the lid closed on his phone he sat there, head hung low kind of shaking it slowly from side-to-side.

When he looked up I thought I could see moisture pooling in the corners of his eyes, although he was trying valiantly to hold it back.

Looking my way he started to say something, thought better of it and stood to leave.

Before he could get out the door, a couple of guys rushed in, almost colliding with him.

"Jason?" one of them said.

With eyes as big as saucers he replied, "Uh...yes. Yes, that's me."

With much apologizing they explained why they had been late and how afraid they had been that he had given up and left.

As they walked over to a vacant table I overheard, "Can I just go ahead and tell you that the job is yours if you want it."

His formerly crestfallen countenance was literally beaming as he stumbled through his acceptance.

Then the oddest thing happened; he excused himself and walked slowly over to where I sat; stood there in silence and then said, "Thanks."

"For what?" said I.

"You know, for being there."

And with that he returned to the table to begin sorting out the terms of his new employment.

As for me, I just sat staring, trying to figure out what had just happened—but, as is often the case, some things are so random they defy explanation.

41

A Good Day

I'M in San Diego for the weekend.

Actually I'm in San Diego every weekend...until my house sells, that is.

Anyway...

I was in a random St. Arbuck's, seated in the corner.

I believe it's called, "Gunfighter's position."

At the table in front of me to the left was a thirty-something blonde woman.

A man of fifty-plus years sat at the table to the right.

They struck up a conversation that, given the proximity, was impossible for me to ignore.

The man's countenance was serene.

I'm not talking about just a feel-good serenity.

This came from the core of his being.

She said, "You're looking rather satisfied and happy today."

To which he replied, "Well, it's a good day to be alive."

"Really?" she said somewhat jadedly. "And what makes this day so special?"

He started to speak; stopped, and pondered for a moment.

"Well, let's just say that given my history, every day is a good day to be alive."

"Care to tell me about it?"

I was glad she asked because I wanted to know myself.

"Sure," he said. "Five years ago I was diagnosed with inoperable lung cancer. They gave me three months to live."

About all she could muster in reply was, "Wow."

"Yeah, the doctors gave me zero chance for survival."

She said, "So, how did you beat it?"

He must have noticed my interest because he looked over at me as if to include me in the conversation.

"I didn't."

She seemed confused.

"What do you mean?"

"I mean that I didn't do anything," he said. Then after a brief pause continued with, "Well, except to tell them that they didn't know what they were talking about. See, I just figured that with a diagnosis like that, I could choose to either lay down and die, or to believe that I was going to live."

"That was how long ago?" she said.

"Five years."

She shook her head slowly and glanced in my direction.

"See, the thing is," he said, "death and I are kind of at a stand-off."

"How so?"

"Well, I know I'm in his cross hairs, but I'm not standing still long enough for him to set his sights on me."

"I don't understand," she said.

"It's like this...death has come to take what's mine, and I'm just not going to give him the satisfaction of going quietly."

"So you're fighting for your life?"

His gaze intensified and he leaned forward in his chair.

"With every bit of strength I have."

She regarded him carefully for a moment and said, "Well, it certainly seems to be working."

He suddenly stood, began gathering up his things and turned to go but turned back at the last second and said, "It is working. But the reason it's working is that I refuse to give up."

She said carefully, "Do you think you've been, well, healed?"

He smiled and said, "I'm not a sick man trying to get well...I'm a healthy man fighting off sickness."

And with that he turned and was gone.

She looked at me...I looked at her and we both kind of shook our heads.

Long after she had left I sat there thinking about those words.

"A healthy man fighting off sickness."

It might be worth a try.

42

The "OB"

SUNDAY afternoon.

My daughter and I are parked at my usual table in a St. Arbuck's in Ocean Beach, sipping our brews and reading the Sunday Union Tribune.

Ocean Beach has historically catered to a Bohemian counter-culture whose residents are, for want of a better word, well, colorful.

I was enjoying my coffee and observing with keen interest the constant parade of skateboarders; young people dressed (or undressed in some instances) in a wide variety of beach attire; bikers on their über customized Harley's; and the occasional old couple out for an afternoon stroll.

Out of the corner of my eye, I spotted two ladies one of whom was pushing a stroller.

They turned toward St. Arbuck's entrance, opened the door and came inside.

Since having grandchildren, I've developed a renewed interest in babies, so I craned my neck toward the stroller to get a better look at their little cutie.

I'm not making this up.

It was a duck!

You heard me.

They had a duck in the stroller.

Enclosed within some sort of zippered netting, but a duck nonetheless.

I said to my daughter, "There's a duck in that stroller."

"Shut up," she said in disbelief.

Once observing the phenomenon for herself, she turned back and said in wide-eyed wonder, "That's crazy!"

We watched as they selected a table and carefully, gently positioned the fowl so he/she/it could be a part of their conversation.

Seriously, I'm not making this up.

One lady went to order some coffee while the other leaned over and, well, started talking to the duck as if it were a cute and cuddly infant.

I looked at my daughter.

She looked at me.

We looked at the ladies who were now fully engaged in whatever they were saying to the creature.

Glancing at the nearest barista I said, "Did you see the duck?"

"The what?" she replied.

I sort of gestured with my head toward the ladies.

"The duck. Over there in that stroller."

"Shut up," she said echoing my daughter's initial reaction.

Stepping out from behind the counter she approached the table and leaned down for a closer look.

Walking back to our table she said, "You're right."

I said, "They talk to it."

She looked at my daughter who nodded her affirmation.

"What exactly do you mean by 'talk'?" she said.

My daughter said, "Like it was a baby or something."

We all turned our gaze toward the duck-women and, sure enough, they were making faces and, uh, cooing noises.

"That's sick!" said the barista. "I'm going to tell my manager."

With that, she walked away.

I said, "That is possibly the most random thing I've ever seen."

"I think that's a cat stroller," my daughter said after a couple minutes of silence.

"A cat stroller?"

"You know, so people can take their cats for a walk."

I decided to leave that one alone as the thought was simply too weird for me to handle at the moment.

"If they take that thing out and start petting it, I'm outta' here," I said.

The manager came out from the back and stood by our table.

"Is there really a duck in there?"

"Yeah," I said. "Go see for yourself."

He walked over and cleaned off a nearby table, spotted the duck, turned back toward me and rolled his eyes.

I couldn't hear what he said to the two ladies, but whatever it was seemed to be quite displeasing to them as their expressions hardened and they glanced at the pampered fowl as if considering covering he/she/its ears so he/she/it wouldn't have to hear what the nasty man was saying.

Without a word they stood and stormed out of St. Arbuck's pushing the stroller so violently the poor duck was forced to utter several expressions of complaint.

The manager said, "Dude, that was totally random."

"You can say that again," I replied.

"Dude, that was..."

"I was kidding."

"Oh," he said and went back to work.

Out on the sidewalk the two ladies squatted by the stroller and seemed to be offering consolation to the duck who, for his/her/its part seemed to be terribly upset by the experience.

I said, "Maybe the duck is all they have."

"Whatever," said my daughter. "They still don't have to push the poor thing around in a stroller."

Having calmed the duck, they walked away down the sidewalk, drawing looks of curiosity and disbelief from passersby.

Just another day in the OB.

43

Conversations With Eddie-Part 7

H E walked through the doorway of St. Arbuck's.
A handsome African-American man in his mid to late
thirties.

His head was shaved.

He looked good.

Confident.

Like he didn't have a care in the world.

He looked like...

Wait a minute!

Impossible!

He looked like...

It was Eddie!

My disgustingly good-looking, African-American best
friend.

He of the shoulder length dreadlocks.

Gone.

He spied me sitting in my usual place in the corner, smiled
and sauntered in my direction.

163

"Happy to see me?" he said as he folded his long, lean frame into the chair.

Staring at his shaven cranium I said, "Uh...you...uh..."

"Yeah, man, cut it all off...just like," he snapped his fingers, "that."

"So, what...you didn't think about it...you just did it?"

"Like I said."

"But...why?"

Wrinkling his brow, he said, "Why not?"

"I don't know. I'm just asking."

"Man don't have to have a reason to shave his head," he said defensively forming his face into one of his famous pouts.

I said, "Yeah, well, if a guy has the kind of hair you have one would think there'd be a reason to chop it off."

He shook his head slowly, blew out a long breath and said, "Just felt the need for a change is all."

"Well, you certainly got that. What does Sylvie think?"

His eyes widened and he looked from side to side saying in a whisper, "She don't know about it yet."

Having raised my cup of coffee halfway to my lips I stopped and stared at him over the rim.

"You're kidding, right?"

A look of pure terror hijacked his normally serene countenance.

"There's gonna' be trouble, I just know it."

I said, "I mean, yeah...what'd you expect? It's not like this is a subtle change."

"Wasn't goin' for subtle."

"Obviously."

He paused for a few seconds and said, "So, you gonna' come with me when I let her see it for the first time?"

I nearly choked on the sip I had just taken.

"Are you crazy? Why would I want to do that?"

"Because we best friends, and best friends watch each other's backs."

"The only back I'd be watching would be yours as you ran away and left me there by myself to deal with her like the time when you bought that Hummer!"

He said petulantly, "I took it back."

We both watched as the workers who are remodeling our St. Arbuck's struggled to get a new pastry case into place.

"Look," I said. "What you need to do is call her up at work and warn her in advance."

"And say what?" He pantomimed talking on his cell phone, 'Hi baby...just wanted to tell you that I's as bald as RG. Have a nice day.'"

"It's a start."

"Dude..." he said miserably. "What have I done!"

I smiled broadly and said, "Seems to me you just provided yourself with an opportunity to work on your communication skills."

He slumped in his chair as the store manager walked by and did a double-take.

"You...your...uh..."

"What? It's just a haircut!" he said while catching his reflection in the store window.

"No," she said, "a haircut is what my husband gets every fourth Tuesday. This is an extreme makeover." She started to turn away but turned back and said to me, "Does his wife know?"

I shook my head with the same expression on my face I could imagine using had someone just asked me if a terminally ill patient was going to make it.

"Dude..." she said, "Oh, dude..." and walked away.

With a look of pure panic he said, "So, what am I gonna' do?"

"Well, there's that wig shop down at the Forum Shops."

"Man," he said, "sometimes you just pure evil, you know that?"

I started to respond but his eyes suddenly lit upon something through the window that drained the color from his handsome face.

"Oh, my sweet lord," he said.

I turned to follow his gaze.

And there walking jauntily toward the entrance was Sylvie and two of her co-workers.

There was nowhere to hide, indeed, there was no time to do anything but sit still and await our mutual destruction.

Sylvie came in first, spotted me and started to wave; then saw Eddie and stopped dead cold in her tracks, her mouth working to form words, but speech had fled.

Walking slowly toward us, she stared at Eddie who seemed as if he were trying to press his body through the wall and into the adjoining establishment.

"Hi, baby," he said weakly...pitifully.

Slowly, almost imperceptibly her mouth began to form into a beautiful smile for which she is famous.

"My, my, my," she said while reaching out and rubbing his head slowly. "Don't you just look fine."

"I...I do?" he stammered.

"Mm-hmmmm. I can't tell you how long I've wanted you to get rid of those stinky ol' dreadlocks."

"Serious? And you're not mad that I did it without tellin' you?"

Laughing she said, "Of course not. Just like I knew you wouldn't be mad when I bought...this new bracelet."

Holding out her hand, she showed us a tennis bracelet that had to have cost at least a thousand dollars—which Eddie could well afford, but still...

He was speechless.

To me she said, "I found the hair in the trash before I left the house for work," and then walked away to join her co-workers at the counter.

He stared at me as if in shock.

"Ummm," I said, "That worked out well."

44

Hair Happens

HOW'S that mocha?

My beloved and I sat contentedly on the patio of St. Arbuck's enjoying what would turn out to be the last nice morning of the year.

She swallowed slowly, savoring the taste and said with a smile, "I think I'm beginning to develop a taste for it."

For those of you not in the know, after a lifetime of resistance, futile though it was, she has recently become as one with caffeine.

And the heavens rejoiced.

And the crowd went wild.

"Yay."

Leaning forward she peered at me in that manner known to married men far and wide.

No...it wasn't "the look," but rather its second cousin, "the exploratory gaze."

This typically occurs when the woman in question has spotted something on the person of the man in question that, in her opinion, does not belong.

"What?" I said while feeling the cold tendrils of fear winding their way around my spine.

Smiling sweetly she said, "Oh, nothing. I was just wondering whether you wanted me to braid that ear hair for you."

Almost of its own accord, my hand flew upward in a hasty attempt the cover the offending ear.

"Hair?" I wailed. "I have hair in my ear?"

"Ears, dear. Make that 'ears'...plural."

I sat there feeling around in my auditory canals with both hands like some guy adjusting his hearing aids.

"Hair in my ears!" I said disgustedly. "I can't believe it."

She waved to a cute little girl proudly drinking hot chocolate with her father and said, "Oh, I don't know why not. I mean it's not like that's the only place."

Dear lord!

"What's that supposed to mean?"

She raised one eyebrow, wiggled her nose and turned her attention back to the sudoku puzzle.

"My nose?" I cried. "There's hair in my nose?"

"Thanks for the info, buddy," said a friendly, eavesdropping guy at the next table.

Ignoring his commentary I said, "But why there? Why not on my head? I mean who needs hair in their flippin' ears anyway?"

A hoary-headed elder stepped slowly and past our table, a veritable forest protruding from ears, nose, eyebrows...

Without looking up she said, "That's you in thirty years."

"Excuse me," I said rising quickly and making my way to the restroom where, after the door was securely locked behind me, I dashed to the mirror and gazed intently at my much-maligned image.

To my horror, it was all true.

Every bit of it...and more!

Turning toward the door I composed my face into a reasonable facsimile of a pleasant expression and exited, making my way quickly back to the table hoping against hope that I wouldn't see anyone I knew.

The coast, as they say, whoever "they" are, was clear.

"So," I said casually, "you going to help me with this?"

Looking up from the puzzle my wife said as if in amazement, "Are you asking for my help? Because if you are I need to call the kids, my sisters, friends, heck, alert the media..."

"Okay, okay," I said. "Point made, point taken." After a brief pause I continued, "I repeat...are you going to help me with this?"

"Oh, sure," she said casually with a wave of her hand and then went back to the puzzle.

From across the patio came a cheerful, lilting, "Hey guys."

It was one of my wife's friends who, by the way, was making her way energetically and cheerfully toward where we sat.

"Great!" said I. "This is just great. What am I supposed to do now?"

Beloved smiled and said, "Just tell her hair happens. She's married...she'll understand."

In the words of Danny DeVito, *"I'll tell you one thing, it's a cruel, cruel world."*

Ain't it just.

45

La Petite Princess

I sat there at my usual place in St. Arbuck's experiencing the same empty-headed stupor that had assailed me most of the week, sipping coffee while watching busy people come and go in a kind of spontaneously synchronized rhythm.

But even they seemed dull.

Nothing was interesting.

Perhaps it was the holiday.

With Christmas a little more than one week away, the proximity seemed to have everyone rushing about under the relentless prod of "Christmas Spirit."

Peace on earth could wait for another day.

There were presents to buy!

Pies to bake.

Stockings to fill.

I had just closed my eyes and buried my face in my hands when I heard a small, almost angelic voice say, "I have a dress."

I looked up and found that the dulcet tones belonged to a little blonde-haired girl of perhaps four or five.

She stood by my table, doing that swinging-your-torso-back-and-forth-with-hands-clasped-behind-your-back little girl thing and gazing innocently at me as if awaiting a response to her pronouncement.

"Why, yes you do," said I as a smile crawled its way onto my previously dour countenance.

She kind of tilted her head to one side and said, "My daddy says I look like a princess."

My smile grew broader.

"Is that right?"

She nodded her head as a shy smile appeared.

She wasn't a particularly pretty child and her handmade dress seemed poorly sewn.

Someone had made a valiant effort to tame her mane of unruly hair—painfully evident was the fact that the hair had eventually won.

And yet, there was a sweetness in her that was compelling.

Glancing past her I noticed a thirty-something man waiting in line to place his order.

By the frequent looks cast my way, I assumed that he was the little girl's father.

The vanquished hair warrior, no doubt.

After a minute or two, he seemed to decide that I was a decent sort and presented no threat to his child.

"Is that your daddy over there?" I asked, pointing to the man.

She nodded quickly after a brief glance in his direction.

I said, "Are you two buying something to take home to your mommy?"

She stared blankly at me for what seemed like an eternity and then with her lower lip trembling slightly she said, "My mommy is in heaven."

Dear God!

"Oh, I'm so sorry, honey," I said.

Yes, I know my response was woefully insufficient, but what could I say, indeed, what could anyone say?

Fanning out the sides of the dress she said, "Mommy made it for me to wear in our church's Christmas program."

In an effort to avoid further clichéd and hackneyed drivel, I simply nodded my head in silent understanding.

"She wanted to be here for Christmas, but God took her to heaven last week."

My heart felt ready to burst.

I wanted to pick that precious child up, cradle her in my arms and tell her whatever she needed to hear that would bring comfort and hope.

She said, "Why did God take my mommy?"

A sniveling voice somewhere inside my mind hissed, *Come on, Mr. big-shot writer. You're so clever, say something to the kid that'll make the pain go away.*

"Well, sweetheart," I said, struggling for composure, "sometimes God gets lonely for his special children—so lonely He just can't stand to be away from them so He...He brings them home."

She nodded silently as if, along with me, weighing the truth of my statement.

After a moment or two, she said softly, "Mister?"

"Yes?" said I, my voice choked with emotion.

"Do you really think I look like a princess?"

Her gaze was piercingly direct.

I blinked my eyes rapidly, hoping by doing so the river of tears pressing against its levy could be held in check.

"Honey," I said. "You are the prettiest little princess I have ever seen." And I meant every word.

I sensed her father's presence before I saw him.

"Megan, come on. You don't want to be late for your program, do you?"

Pointing my direction she said proudly, "Daddy, this man thinks I'm the prettiest little princess he's ever seen."

As he stood just behind her, holding a coffee in one hand

and hot chocolate in the other, our eyes met, this brave father's and mine.

And while no words were spoken, understanding passed between us.

That and something more—gratitude.

Then with his lips pressed together in a tight smile, he said, "And did you say thank-you?"

Megan looked at me and said bashfully, "Thank-you."

They turned to go and almost made it out the door when suddenly Megan ran back and threw her arms about my neck hugging me tightly.

And then she was gone.

Me, I was left breathless with the wonder of what had just transpired.

I sat there not knowing what to do.

And then suddenly I knew exactly what to do.

I quickly threw my things into my trendy European man-purse and ran out the door.

I had a Christmas program to see, and if I hurried, I could probably catch the little princess and her father in the parking lot and get directions.

All at once, Christmas had taken on a whole new meaning.

46

The Color Of Love

I T was predictably hectic at St. Arbuck's with customers coming and going in a nearly unbroken chain of poor souls whose morning just wouldn't be complete without the obsessive indulgence.

According to the neighborhood weather (available by dialing a three digit number on a land-line) by 7:30 AM the mercury was still hovering around forty-five degrees, not atypical for the first of March, but a bit too chilly for my taste.

That's Vegas for you: we long for the cold of winter when it's summer, and then all winter long all you hear is, "Well, it'll warm up soon."

I opened my laptop and was just about to dive into writing when a young couple came through the door.

He, Caucasian and she, African-American.

Both extremely good-looking.

Well dressed, as if enjoying the fruits of financial success.

He had piercing blue eyes and light brown hair and she that rare combination of facial features that lent an exotic and mysterious quality to her appearance.

While they searched for a place to sit, two children, both under the age of two, contended for their parent's attention.

An empty table was chosen a short distance from my usual corner spot and the parents began off-loading kids and enough baggage to justify a cross-country trip.

It made me remember the days when it required just as much effort to make a five minute trip to the convenience store as it did to make a trip lasting several hours.

Now that I think about it, the long trip was actually much easier.

Anyway...

They got everyone settled—a statement that begs the question of whether "settled" is something parents of young children ever get to experience.

To be accurate, I should say that everyone was settled except for the little girl, she of the oh-so-cute pigtails and impossibly large brown eyes which, oddly enough, happened to be locked onto me at that moment.

The father took his wife's order for a mocha latte, the little girl's order for milk and headed for the counter.

At least I think the little girl ordered milk.

Actually I couldn't be certain, for what I had interpreted as "Milk," could just as easily have been interpreted as, "Moke; Meek; Mao; Muck" or one of several other vocabulary annihilations.

The other child, a baby of no more than five or six months, began to squall prompting the mother to reach for a bottle from the most high-tech diaper bag I'd ever seen.

By then the father had returned and the four sat in familial bliss sipping their beverages of choice, simply comfortable being together.

It was then that I found my imagination captured by something.

I began to look at those children wondering how I would describe them to my wife.

I mean they weren't Caucasian.

But they weren't African-American either.

How does one ascribe a color to offspring such as these?

And then I knew.

It had been right in front of me all the time.

Those two adorable little children were *the color of love*—love between a man and a woman manifested in their progeny.

The little girl turned part-way around in her seat, pointed at me and said in her tiny little girl voice, "Poppa."

I heard her mother say, "You think that man looks like your grandpa?"

As if in answer, she turned around again as if to make sure, pointed my way and repeated, "Poppa."

She then climbed down from her seat and ran over to where I sat, looked up at me in infinite cuteness and proceeded to start talking up a storm.

Not that I understood a single word, but to be polite I lobbed a few well-placed, "Really?" "Is that right?" "You don't say?" replies which kept her going for a good ten minutes.

Finally, the father walked over, scooped up his treasure and said with wink and a smile, "We're, uh, working on her shyness."

"Right," I said knowingly as the two rejoined the mother and little brother.

Over the course of the next thirty minutes I was so captivated by that beautiful little family that I didn't get a scrap of work done.

"The color of love."

"Excuse me?" said an industrious barista who happened to be wiping the table next to mine.

I didn't realize I had spoken the phrase out loud.

"Oh, nothing," said I dismissively hoping I wouldn't have to explain myself.

Thankfully, she moved off to another table leaving me to my musings.

While we were sleeping a whole, new race has been born here in the midst of our years.

They are children who are neither black nor white, yellow nor brown but children of a different color.

The color of love.

And to quote the late Charlie Chaplin, "What a wonderful world."

RG...out!

Author's Notes

J UST a few brief words about the writing of "Snapshots At St. Arbuck's."

My love for coffee had its genesis back in high school when my buddies and I would gather at a neighborhood diner and order up a good stiff brew—which, for the record, we hated at the time but were far too manly to admit it.

We would sit for hours drinking and talking, in no particular hurry to be anywhere except with each other.

The practice continued throughout my collegiate years. Of course, the location had changed and I was with a different set of friends, but the core activity, that of warm and lingering conversation, remained the same.

Marriage, family and career intruded, as they most often do, and my world became a dizzying maze of schedules and pressures which left time for little else except keeping my head above water.

Added to that was the slow but certain demise of the neighborhood diner, which historically had been a community gathering place.

Then one day I spotted my very first St. Arbuck's.

It was in San Diego, California.

Having just completed my morning work-out routine, a friend and I were on our way to get donuts.

I know...it doesn't make any sense.

It's not supposed to make sense.

It's a donut thing.

He spotted the now famous sign and said, "Hey, my sister had coffee there the other day and she said it was great."

So we decided to check it out.

It quickly brought back memories of simpler, happier times.

The smells.

The sounds.

The sight of people relaxing around tables, engaged in conversation and listening to some pretty good music on the in-store sound system.

It immediately became our regular morning place.

That was a while ago now.

Over time, St. Arbuck's has become *my* place.

I seek it out wherever I live or travel.

While factual, I crafted the preceding stories with sufficient literary and dramatic license to protect the identities of all persons either living or dead as well as the various locations.

So if you see someone who looks a little familiar, it is more than likely pure coincidence.

There are so many more stories to tell.

So much more hope to absorb.

That said, I think I need a cuppa' Joe.

Thanks for reading.

R.G. Ryan

Acknowledgements

THERE are so many who have abandoned hope, laid their dreams to rest and settled for existence when they were meant to live deeply, richly. The truth is we have choices. Either we can dream of living a great life, or we can start living our great dream. I am one who has made the choice to live and this book is a tangible expression of that choice.

There are some folks who I need to thank with expressions of deep and heartfelt gratitude for without their inspiration and tireless efforts, this book would not exist.

First and foremost, Cheri, the wife of my youth, the companion of my middle years. It's been worth it—each and every step of the journey. Thank-you for standing your ground in editing and not backing down from my tantrums.

My daughter Sarah for being so grammatically correct and her husband, Brett, for letting me crash at their beachside bungalow.

My son, Ryan—his wife, LaVonda and the two cutest grandkids on earth, Ocean and Diego—for his ceaseless affirmation in telling me that I could do this.

Ken Blanchard for his expert advice, kindness, wisdom and fabulously written foreword. Thank-you for believing in this project. Your kind words of encouragement got me through many hard times.

Danny Gans for being such a great friend, supporter and for introducing me to Ken.

Thank-you as well to those faithful inhabitants of my *vox* neighborhood who have tirelessly encouraged me along this journey.

And, Eddie Washington, wherever you are, your contribution has been incalculable. BTW, you owe me lunch.

Also from Dream Chasers Media Group:

By Strangers Quickly Told

A novel by

R.G. Ryan

You can never truly experience great loss unless you have first known great love.

Set in 1947 against the backdrop of post-war America, *By Strangers Quickly Told* is the story of Maggie Wheeler—an Ozark mountain maiden who loved Clark Gable—and her lifelong dream of living in New York City. It follows Maggie on her journey from being the daughter of a poor, Arkansas sharecropper to her life as a nanny for a wealthy Irish family in the big city and her subsequent love affair with a popular jazz musician.

It is a story of dreams born and dreams shattered; love found and love snatched too quickly away; of hope lost and hope restored. And in the end, Maggie finds that wherever there is misery, mercy is close by.

COMING SOON:

Snapshots At St. Arbuck's Vol. II